Bracing o   he bathtub, Le   eam over her th   into her skin, working downward to her feet before moving to the other leg.

She swallowed, licking her lips. Staring at herself in the mirror, she began rubbing the mango butter over her belly. Her muscles quivered, tightened. She paused, then slowly slid her hands up to her breasts. An odd, tingling awareness rippled over her skin.

Then, without warning, the bathroom doorknob began to turn. A moment later Quentin stood in the doorway, his lids at half-mast over his smoldering hazel eyes. Their gazes locked in the mirror.

Without a word he started toward her, a slow, stealthy advance that made her pulse hammer.

When he'd reached the tub where she stood, he dipped his fingers into the jar of cream, scooping out enough to coat both of his hands. Her body hummed with arousal. He moved behind her, staring at their joined reflections in the mirror. Then a slow, sensual smile curved his mouth before he reached out to touch her.

Books by Maureen Smith

Kimani Romance

A Legal Affair
A Guilty Affair
A Risky Affair
Secret Agent Seduction
Touch of Heaven
Recipe for Temptation
Tempt Me at Midnight

Kimani Arabesque

With Every Breath
A Heartbeat Away

MAUREEN SMITH

is the author of sixteen novels and one novella. She received a B.A. in English from the University of Maryland with a minor in creative writing. She is a former freelance writer whose articles were featured in various print and online publications. Since the release of her debut novel in 2002, Maureen has been nominated for three *RT Book Reviews* Reviewers' Choice Awards and fourteen Emma Awards, and she has won the Romance in Color Reviewers' Choice Awards for New Author of the Year and Romantic Suspense of the Year. Her novel *Secret Agent Seduction* won the 2010 Emma Award for Best Romantic Suspense.

Maureen lives in San Antonio, Texas, with her husband, two children and a miniature schnauzer. She loves to hear from readers and can be reached at author@maureen-smith.com. Please visit her website at www.maureen-smith.com for news about her upcoming releases.

Tempt me at
MIDNIGHT

Maureen Smith

KIMANI
ROMANCE

For Lonnie, Brianna, and MJ
The best niece and nephews in the world

KIMANI PRESS™

Recycling programs
for this product may
not exist in your area.

ISBN-13: 978-0-373-86191-0

TEMPT ME AT MIDNIGHT

Copyright © 2010 by Maureen Smith

www.kimanipress.com

Printed in U.S.A.

Dear Reader,

In my previous novel, *Recipe for Temptation,* you were introduced to wickedly irresistible Quentin Reddick. With his killer looks, lazy smile and magnetic charm, Quentin is a bona fide ladies' man who has no intention of ever settling down. That is, until he locks lips with his best friend, Lexi Austin, at a New Year's Eve party. After that magical night, all bets are off.

I've always been a sucker for stories that feature friends turned lovers. What could be more romantic than falling madly in love with the one person who knows you better than anyone else? That's what Quentin and Lexi are about to find out.

I hope you will enjoy their passionate journey, which begins with a stolen kiss at the stroke of midnight....

As always, please share your thoughts with me at author@maureen-smith.com.

Until next time, happy New Year and happy reading!

Maureen Smith

Chapter 1

The grand ballroom was a sea of masks. Black, white, sequined and feathered masks everywhere Lexi Austin looked.

As she waded through the crowd of revelers, excitement pulsed through her veins. In half an hour the clock would strike twelve, ushering in a new year. Lexi could think of no better way to celebrate than by attending a masquerade ball at a luxurious château owned by legendary fashion designer Asha Dubois. The glitzy soiree was the hottest ticket in France every year, attended by everyone who was anyone in the fashion industry. Which meant that Lexi could be rubbing elbows with the likes of Miuccia Prada and John Galliano without even—

A man in a feathered black mask suddenly jostled her, murmuring apologetically, *"Excusez-moi."*

Lexi smiled beneath the jeweled white mask that covered

the upper half of her own face. *"Ce n'est pas grave,"* she assured him, the words rolling smoothly off her tongue.

The stranger returned her smile before moving off.

Lexi continued across the crowded room, taking in the sights and sounds as if she'd just arrived at the party. A canopy of twinkling lights hung from the frescoed ceiling, and ornate wall tapestries and marble columns evoked the grandeur of the French Renaissance. A fifteen-piece orchestra performed a dreamy Viennese waltz that had lured many couples onto the dance floor, the swirl of white ball gowns transforming the scene into a shimmering fairyland.

As Lexi paused to watch the dancers, she couldn't help wishing she had a date that evening. What could be more romantic than ringing in the New Year wrapped in the arms of a man she loved?

But she'd been woefully unlucky in that department, so tonight she was flying solo.

A soft smile curved her mouth when two of her closest friends, Michael and Reese Wolf, whirled into her line of sight. Michael was darkly handsome in a black tuxedo, while Reese was positively radiant in a long white gown that flowed gently over her round, protruding belly. Being eight months pregnant hadn't slowed her down that evening; her head was thrown back in laughter as her husband twirled her gracefully around the dance floor.

As Lexi watched the happy couple, she thought of the missing member of their group. Quentin Reddick had called last night to let them know he'd be unable to join them in France, citing an unexpected development in one of his upcoming court cases. Lexi had been sorely disappointed. Quentin was her best friend. Over the years they'd attended numerous parties together, often serving as each other's "mock date."

Not that Quentin ever had any trouble finding *real* dates, Lexi thought wryly. The man was a veritable chick magnet. If he'd been at tonight's ball, he would have spent the evening surrounded by gorgeous, leggy supermodels. God knows there were plenty in attendance.

Still, despite his popularity with the ladies, Lexi had always known she could count on Quentin to save her a dance or two. When she returned home to Atlanta in a few days, she'd be sure to give him an earful for abandoning her.

With one last envious glance at the dancing couples, Lexi made her way across the ballroom toward a row of French doors that opened onto an ivy-draped terrace. She'd decided to ring in the New Year outside on the balcony, which was preferable to remaining indoors, where she'd be surrounded by couples kissing and embracing at the stroke of midnight.

When she reached the doors to the terrace, she was relieved to see that it was deserted. The cool temperature had undoubtedly deterred the other guests from wandering out there to steal a romantic moment under the stars or enjoy the breathtaking view of rolling green hills, beautifully landscaped gardens and lush vineyards.

Standing at the white stone balustrade, Lexi closed her eyes and inhaled the crisp night air. She almost imagined she could detect the scents of lavender and fermenting grapes that would permeate the French countryside during warmer months.

She'd been thrilled when Michael and Reese invited her to celebrate the New Year with his family in France. Lexi would have been content to spend the holiday with her friends anywhere. Never in her wildest dreams could she have imagined staying at a sprawling twenty-bedroom château nestled deep in the country's most famous wine region. Burgundy was a chef's paradise, a French mecca for lovers of gourmet cuisine and exquisite wine. Lexi couldn't *wait* to go exploring tomorrow.

Belatedly, she realized that the orchestra had stopped playing inside the ballroom. An air of hushed excitement swept over the crowd moments before Asha Dubois's lilting, cultured voice came over the loudspeaker. "*Bonsoir, mes amis.* I hope all of you are having a splendid time this evening."

She paused, chuckling softly as a chorus of cheers and applause went around the room. "*Très bien.* I'm very pleased to hear it. Well, my dear friends, we're just minutes away from welcoming a new year. If you haven't already, please be sure to take a flute of champagne from one of the servers circulating around the room. After all, darlings, you can't toast the New Year empty-handed."

Glancing down at her empty hands clasped over the balustrade, Lexi smiled ruefully.

"For those of you who have never attended one of my masquerade balls," Asha continued, "we observe a very simple tradition. At the stroke of midnight, everyone removes their masks and reveals themselves. So without further ado, I'd like to wish all of you a wonderful New Year. May you experience love, laughter and joy—and have plenty of hot, mind-blowing sex!"

Lexi grinned as the crowd roared with laughter and approval. And then the revelers joined together to belt out the last ten seconds of the countdown: "…five, four, three, two—"

As fireworks erupted into the night sky, a pair of strong arms curved around Lexi's waist and swept her around. She had only a fleeting glimpse of a black mask and impossibly broad shoulders before the stranger lowered his head.

She gasped at the shock of soft, warm lips covering hers.

Her first instinct was to jerk away. But the sudden onslaught of pleasure engulfing her body made it impossible for her to move.

The stranger increased the pressure of his mouth against hers as his hands slid up her back, holding her close against his hard, muscular frame. Dazedly her mind registered that he was very tall, at least six-five. And he tasted delicious—an irresistible combination of chocolate, peppermint and man. Her blood ignited, and her heart thundered furiously.

The stranger, whoever he was, could kiss like *no* other man she'd ever kissed before. As he traced the shape of her lips with his tongue, violent pulses of sensation charged through her body. She opened her mouth and his tongue dipped inside, lazily stroking hers. A tiny sound caught in her throat, a whimper of pleasure.

He deepened the kiss, exploring her mouth with slow, sensual licks that left her quaking all over. She arched against him, craving more.

All too soon, he released her and lifted his head.

Disoriented, Lexi swayed on her feet before strong hands gently gripped her upper arms, steadying her. She opened her eyes slowly.

"Happy New Year." A deep, familiar voice greeted her.

Lexi went rigid, her eyes widening with shock. No, it couldn't be. *"Quentin?"*

Slowly he reached up and removed his mask. A kaleidoscope of bright colors flashed across his wickedly handsome face—a face Lexi knew almost as well as her own.

She staggered backward, stunned and shaken. "Wh-what the hell do you think you're doing?"

"Wishing you a Happy New Year," Quentin murmured.

"You couldn't do that *without* kissing me?" she cried in exasperated disbelief.

Another burst of fireworks illuminated the devilish gleam in his hazel eyes. "Come now," he drawled. "What's a little kiss between old friends?"

Lexi gaped at him. There'd been nothing remotely "little" about that kiss. Good Lord, her knees were still knocking together!

"That wasn't some chaste peck on the lips, Quentin," she said darkly. "You *French-kissed* me."

His eyes glimmered with amusement. "We're in France."

"So what!"

One broad shoulder shrugged. "When in France…"

Lexi shook her head, her eyes narrowing suspiciously on his face. "Have you been drinking?"

"No," Quentin said with a laugh, slipping his hands into his pants pockets. He looked like a million bucks in a classic black tuxedo that fit his body like a dream.

"What're you doing here anyway?" Lexi grumbled. "I thought you couldn't make it."

"Things changed."

"Like what?"

Instead of answering, he took a step toward her.

Alarmed, Lexi backed away until she came up against the stone balustrade. Trapped, she stared up at him, afraid he might try to kiss her again. "Quentin—"

"Relax." He reached out, gently pulling her mask off her face. She'd completely forgotten she was wearing one, and now she felt utterly exposed without it.

Quentin set the mask down on the banister. His lazy

gaze raked over her, taking in the low neckline and cinched waist of her strapless white gown before sliding back up to her face. "You look beautiful, Lex," he murmured.

"Thanks." She inhaled deeply, appalled by how uneven her breath was, how hard it was to draw air into her lungs. "Asha had gowns designed for me, Reese and Samara. I really lucked out by having a close friend whose stepmother is a famous fashion mogul."

Quentin's eyes glinted wickedly. "That was one helluva toast she made. Words to live by."

At the memory of Asha's admonition to her guests to have "plenty of hot, mind-blowing sex," Lexi flushed deeply—a reaction that confused her. Normally she would have laughed and made some quip about Quentin's notoriously overactive sex life.

But tonight she could only manage a noncommittal "hmm."

Inside the ballroom, the orchestra was playing an extended version of "Auld Lang Syne" as the unmasked partygoers milled around laughing, shaking hands and exchanging good wishes. Some had drifted toward the French doors to watch the fireworks display. No one attempted to join the two occupants of the terrace.

Lexi dragged in another deep breath, striving for composure. "When did you arrive?" she asked Quentin.

"About half an hour ago." Smiling, he touched her face. "I've been looking for you ever since."

She swallowed hard. "Yeah?"

"Yeah."

"Well, you found me." *Had he ever!* "Now you can get back to the party. In case you haven't noticed, there's a roomful of supermodels who are just waiting to be debauched. As a matter of fact, one of them just walked by. I think you caught her eye, Quentin."

She waited for him to take the bait and glance over his shoulder to catch a glimpse of the woman in question. To her surprise, his gaze never strayed from hers.

Frowning, Lexi reached up and laid her hand across his forehead as if to check his temperature. "Sweetie, are you feeling okay?"

He chuckled softly. "I feel fine."

"Are you sure? You don't seem like yourself. Maybe you're jet-lagged. Or—"

"Maybe I'm just happy to see you," he finished.

The warm, husky undertone of his voice skated along her nerve endings and quickened her heart rate.

She gave him a wobbly smile. "I'm happy to see you too, Quentin."

And she really was. She just wished they hadn't gotten off to such a nerve-racking start. That kiss… *Oh, God.* If that searing kiss was any indication of Quentin's prowess as a lover, it was no wonder he couldn't keep women out of his bed.

"You owe me a dance," he told her.

Lexi shook her head quickly—maybe too quickly. But she couldn't help it. The thought of being in his arms again scared her senseless. "Sorry, but you'll have to take a rain check. My feet are killing me in these heels."

"So take 'em off."

"Wouldn't do much good. The damage has already been done. Besides, I was planning to cut out soon anyway. Asha had me and the girls running around Paris all day, so I'm exhausted." To demonstrate, she covered her mouth to stifle what she hoped was a convincingly huge yawn.

Quentin tsk-tsked her. "Spoilsport."

She grinned. "Hey, it's not my fault you got here late. But don't worry. I'm leaving you in good hands. The supermodel I just mentioned? Don't look now, but she's back. And it's a damn good thing we're not involved, Q, or I'd have to kick her ninety-pound ass for stalking my man."

Laughing, Quentin sent a lazy glance over his shoulder. The gorgeous woman, slim and exquisitely tall, hovered near the terrace doors. She met Quentin's gaze, smiled coyly and fluttered her fingers in a wave.

He flashed her a smile before returning his attention to Lexi. "I'm staying in the room next to yours." Which was the *last* thing she wanted to hear. "If you're still awake when I come up, maybe we can play cards or something."

Lexi forced out a laugh. "Trust me, I won't be awake. And something tells me you won't be thinking about cards by the time you make it back to your room," she added with a meaningful glance over his shoulder.

Quentin shifted closer. "Lex—"

"Oh, look, there's Michael and Reese!" she exclaimed, grateful for the distraction. "They told me they'd be heading to bed right after midnight. I'll walk out with them. Good night, sweetie." Pressing a quick kiss to Quentin's smooth-shaven cheek, she slipped from between him and the balustrade and hurried across the terrace.

Although she was retiring early, she didn't expect to get much sleep. The memory of Quentin's kiss would keep her awake tonight, and for many nights to come.

Chapter 2

The last thought Quentin had before falling asleep was the same thought that greeted him when he woke up the next morning: he'd kissed Lexi.

In the light of day his behavior seemed surreal, like something he'd only imagined. Except he'd never imagined doing something as reckless as what he'd done last night. To Lexi. His best friend. A woman who'd always been more like a sister to him than anything else.

But there was nothing *brotherly* about the way he'd felt when he pulled her into his arms and kissed her. She'd tasted sweeter than he could ever have imagined, and the feel of her petite, curvy body pressed against his had tempted him beyond all reason.

The scary part was, he hadn't even intended to kiss her when he'd found her on the terrace last night. True, he'd tracked her down with a single-minded focus, bulldozing his way through the crowd in order to reach her before the clock struck twelve. And true, something had clutched in his chest when he saw her standing alone at the balcony, looking ethereally beautiful in that white goddess gown. But even then, as he'd stood in the doorway gazing at her, he'd only intended to sneak up behind her and whisper in her ear, "Happy New Year!"

But as he strode across the terrace, something came over him. Before he realized what he was doing, he was grabbing her, then kissing her. And it felt so damn good he hadn't wanted to stop.

Swearing under his breath, Quentin rolled over in the king-size bed and frowned up at the ceiling.

What the hell have you done, Reddick?

He and Lexi had been best friends for over twenty years. In all that time he'd never made a move on her, even though he'd have to be comatose not to notice what a sweet little number she was. With her beautiful brown skin, lush lips and long-lashed, exotic eyes that could skewer or beguile with a glance, Lexi had always drawn her share of male attention. At parties and nightclubs, she'd never been able to take three steps without some loser trying to grab her hand and lure her onto the dance floor—until he saw Quentin and Michael looming behind her with menacing expressions. The two friends had been protective of Lexi since college, taking her under their wing like a beloved baby sister. Despite their womanizing reputations, she'd trusted them, deeming them safe to befriend.

She meant more to Quentin than any other woman he'd ever known. The last thing he wanted was to jeopardize their friendship because he'd had a moment of temporary insanity. Although Lexi had responded hungrily to his kiss, she'd been stunned and outraged when she discovered that Quentin was behind the mask. For all he knew, she'd spent the rest of the night plotting her revenge by making a voodoo doll of him, which she'd use to inflict pain on him at the worst possible moments. Like when he was arguing a case in court. Or flirting with a beautiful woman.

Chuckling grimly at the thought, Quentin decided to test the waters.

Raising his arm above the headboard, he rapped his knuckle on the wall four times, which was code for: *am I in trouble?*

He waited tensely.

One knock meant he was forgiven. Two knocks meant he was in the doghouse and would have to do some serious groveling to get back into her good graces.

After an agonizing eternity, Lexi responded. *Thump.*

A slow, relieved grin spread across Quentin's face.

Things were back to normal between them. With any luck, they'd stay that way.

Lexi spent a long, restless night tortured by mental replays of the smoldering kiss she and Quentin had shared. But, surprisingly, when she awoke the next morning, she was able to put the whole situation into perspective.

Last night had been an aberration.

The excitement of New Year's Eve, the mystique of a masquerade ball, fireworks cascading over a moonlit balcony—all were the perfect ingredients for a romantic liaison. Who *wouldn't* have gotten caught up in the moment?

She and Quentin were two mature, reasonable adults. They didn't have to throw away their friendship over what amounted to a fluke. An exquisitely passionate fluke—but a fluke nonetheless.

It was time to put the kiss behind her, Lexi decided. Knowing Quentin, he already had.

No sooner had she completed the thought than she heard four distinct knocks on her bedroom wall.

She smiled to herself. Quentin was reaching out to her in their special code language, which they'd cleverly dubbed "LexiQuen" during a spring break trip to Cabo San Lucas, where they'd argued heatedly one evening after Quentin left her stranded at a nightclub.

Just to make him squirm, as she'd done that night many years ago, Lexi took her sweet time before lifting her hand to the wall and knocking once. And then she grinned, imagining the relieved expression on Quentin's face. She never could stay mad at him for very long.

An hour later she emerged from her room, freshly showered and dressed in a cream cashmere sweater and designer jeans. Determined to prove that nothing had changed between her and Quentin, she decided to stop by his room so they could head down to breakfast together.

Before she'd taken two steps his door swung open and out strutted the tall, gorgeous waif from last night's ball. The skimpy dress she wore ended just beneath the curve of her butt and showed off miles of long, slender legs. Her black hair was tousled, as if she'd just risen from Quentin's bed—which she undoubtedly had.

Lexi froze in her tracks, watching as the woman smiled coquettishly and waved at Quentin, who was framed in the doorway, his chest and feet bare. A smile played at the edges of his mouth as he watched her sashay down the hall. When she'd disappeared around the corner, he shook his head in amusement and closed the door.

Inwardly relieved that he hadn't seen her standing there, Lexi ditched the idea of waiting for him and headed downstairs alone.

Just as she'd expected, Quentin had already forgotten about kissing her and was back to his womanizing ways.

So all was right with the world again. Which was exactly what she'd wanted.

Right?

Of course, Lexi thought, annoyed that she was even second-guessing herself. The best thing she could do was pretend that the kiss had never happened. The sooner she put it out of her mind, the better off she'd be.

Easier said than done.

Resolutely ignoring her conscience, Lexi focused on her surroundings. The interior of Asha's château was every bit as impressive as the exterior. As Lexi made her way downstairs, she couldn't help feeling as though she'd been transported back in time to the opulent days of the French royalty. Each room she passed was large and luxuriously appointed with beautiful antique furniture, rich fabrics, soaring fireplaces, original period paintings and priceless tapestries.

The grand marble staircase descended to a cavernous foyer that was lit by a massive crystal chandelier. Lexi followed the sound of laughing voices to a pair of French doors that opened onto an enormous breakfast room. A fire crackled invitingly in the hearth, and bright winter sunlight poured through a row of windows that overlooked the immaculately landscaped grounds of the estate.

Everyone was already gathered around the long mahogany table. At opposite ends were Asha and Sterling Wolf, former adversaries who'd shocked their children last year when they announced that they were getting married. They were as different as night and day, yet no one could dispute that they absolutely belonged together.

As did the other two couples seated at the table. Reese had her head resting on Michael's shoulder as he gently rubbed her swollen stomach, while his younger brother

Marcus couldn't stop smiling at his gorgeous wife, Samara, who sat across from him.

As Lexi entered the sunny room, she was met by a chorus of warm greetings.

"Good morning, everyone." Smiling, she bent and planted an affectionate kiss on Sterling Wolf's clean-shaven dark cheek. He'd always been more like a father to her than the worthless man who'd abandoned her when she was a child. Which was why Sterling had insisted that she call him Dad, and she'd asked him to give her away at her wedding four years ago. In light of the way her disastrous marriage had ended, having Sterling walk her down the aisle was the *only* good decision she'd made that day.

"Where's your partner in crime?" he asked her.

"Still in his room." Lexi slid into the empty chair beside Reese, who gave her a disappointed look. "What?"

"We were counting on you to bring Quentin downstairs," Reese said. "You know he's always late to everything, and the baby and I are starving."

Lexi was mildly alarmed. "You mean you haven't eaten anything yet? It's almost ten o'clock!"

"I had a light snack," Reese admitted with a sheepish grin. "But that's not the point. Whenever we all go out to dinner, you always make sure Quentin gets there on time. That's, like, your designated role."

Lexi shrugged, draping a linen napkin across her lap. "I didn't want to disturb him. He, uh, had a late night."

"Actually," Asha interjected drolly from the other end of the table, "he left the ball half an hour after you did."

Lexi glanced up in surprise. "He did?"

"Oui." Asha held her gaze. "Alone."

Lexi flushed. "Oh," was all she could say.

So maybe the sexy supermodel hadn't spent the night with Quentin. That didn't mean he hadn't slept with her.

Maybe she'd sneaked into his room for a quickie early that morning. And maybe she'd been sound asleep, or in the bathroom, when Quentin sent his coded message to Lexi.

Asha was studying her, a calculating gleam in her dark eyes that made Lexi want to squirm. She remembered Samara once telling her about Asha's uncanny ability to ferret out people's darkest secrets without them uttering a word. Unless Asha had witnessed what transpired on the terrace last night, there was no way she could know that Quentin had kissed Lexi.

Or could she? Lexi wondered uneasily. Was the truth written all over her face?

As she stared at Asha, the other woman's full lips curved in a quiet, intuitive smile. "I'm hoping you'll take my New Year's toast to heart, Alexis," she murmured.

Lexi eyed her warily. "What do you mean?"

"With all due respect, *chère,* my words weren't intended for those of us who are already having plenty of hot, mind-blowing sex."

Scandalized, Samara gasped. "Mom!"

Michael and Marcus groaned at the thought of their sixty-something father *having* sex, let alone steamy sex. But how could he not when he was married to Asha—a tall, voluptuous, stunningly beautiful woman who oozed more sex appeal than most women half her age?

As Sterling chuckled sheepishly, Samara muttered in exasperation, "When other moms make toasts, they wish people health, happiness and prosperity. But not *my* mother. My mother tells a roomful of her guests to get laid."

Asha smiled unrepentantly. "Oh, relax, darling. At least you didn't have to cover any small ears this time."

"Where *are* the twins?" Lexi asked, as much to change

the subject as out of curiosity. If her face got any hotter, her head would combust.

"The boys already ate." Samara chuckled wryly. "They were up at an ungodly hour this morning, pestering me and Marcus to take them exploring around the property. Mom's gardener was kind enough to do the honors."

Lexi grinned. "Given how huge this place is, you won't see your offspring for a while."

The two parents shared a conspiratorial look. "We know."

Laughter went around the table.

"Don't start the party without me," came an amused drawl from the doorway.

Everyone turned as Quentin sauntered into the room with his lazy, rolling swagger. He was dressed in dark jeans that hung low on his hips and a hunter-green turtleneck that molded his wide shoulders and broad, muscular torso. As Lexi stared at him, she remembered the strength of his arms wrapped around her, the hardness of his chest pressed against hers. They'd hugged countless times before, but last night was the first time she'd ever wanted to cling to him, to rub her aching breasts against his body. She wondered if she'd ever be able to look at him again without reliving those heady, forbidden moments in his embrace.

As he approached the table, Michael wagged his head at him. "'Bout time you got here. My wife was seconds away from marching upstairs and dragging you out of your room."

Quentin chuckled. "Damn. My bad." He leaned down to kiss Reese's upturned cheek. "Didn't mean to keep you waiting, baby girl. Forgive me?"

Reese grinned at him. "You're forgiven."

Lexi did a mental eye roll. It seemed that *no* woman was

immune to Quentin Reddick's charms. Not even pregnant, blissfully married women.

Quentin rounded the table and lowered his long body into the chair across from Lexi. As their eyes met, a strange ripple of awareness raced down her spine. The color of his shirt brought out the green flecks in his eyes, making them appear even brighter than usual. Piercing.

When he winked at Lexi, her heart fluttered like the wings of a caged bird. Mortified, she could only muster a feeble smile.

A team of servers bearing hot, fragrant platters of food appeared. Asha's chef had prepared a lavish pancake breakfast, a New Year's Day tradition in France.

As the meal got under way, Lexi found her gaze straying to Quentin as he conversed with Marcus beside him. As though she were seeing him for the very first time, she mentally catalogued heavy black brows, hazel eyes shaded by long straight lashes, a strong blade of a nose, ruthlessly hard cheekbones, a sculpted mouth and a square jaw. His face was far too masculine to ever be considered pretty, though his glorious golden complexion could inspire poetry when it gleamed in the sun—as it did now. He kept his black hair cropped close to his scalp, but whenever it grew out a little, you could detect the wavy texture he'd inherited from his late biracial father.

As her gaze returned to his lips and lingered, Lexi wondered how she'd never noticed just how lush and sensual they were. Her flesh heated at the memory of them moving slowly and possessively over hers, melting her body until she was nothing more than a quivering jumble of need.

Quentin turned his head then, meeting her gaze. An electric current of awareness passed between them.

"What happened to your friend?" Lexi blurted before she could think better of it.

Those glittering eyes narrowed on hers. "Who?"

"If you're talking about Giselle," Asha interjected in an amused voice, "I sent her back to the hotel with my driver."

Although the château was spacious enough to easily accommodate a royal family and a fleet of their servants, Asha had reserved a block of rooms at a local hotel for her overnight guests, most of whom had traveled three hours from Paris to attend the masquerade ball. She'd made no apologies for limiting her houseguests to family members, which, by extension, included Lexi and Quentin.

Taking a sip of her café au lait, Lexi murmured, "Giselle must have been disappointed to leave."

"Perhaps." Asha gave her a meaningful look. "But no woman likes to be a third wheel."

Lexi faltered, wondering whether she or Giselle would have assumed the unenviable role. Considering that it was Giselle who'd sashayed out of Quentin's bedroom that morning, it was a safe bet that *Lexi* would have been the odd one out.

Unsettled by the thought, she returned her attention to her delicious plate of crêpes, making a mental note to pay her compliments to the chef after breakfast. As a graduate of a renowned French culinary school, Lexi could always appreciate a well-executed crêpe—even when she suddenly had no appetite for it.

"I'm so delighted you were able to join us this weekend, Quentin," Asha said warmly. "We were terribly disappointed when you called to say you wouldn't be coming. Alexis took the news especially hard. Not even a day of shopping and sightseeing in Paris could pull her out of her funk."

"Is that right?" Quentin's eyes glinted with amusement over the rim of his coffee cup.

Lexi inwardly groaned, wondering what she could have possibly done to land in Asha's crosshairs that morning.

But a moment later, Asha said to Quentin, "I thought it was quite touching the way you went in search of Alexis as soon as you arrived. My goodness, you barely stopped to greet anyone else." Her dark eyes twinkled. "If I didn't know better, darling, I would think you rushed here just to be with Alexis."

Silence descended over the table as the others exchanged amused, considering glances.

Heart thudding, Lexi stared at Quentin and he stared back, neither denying nor confirming Asha's suspicion.

Eager to defuse the strange tension between them, Lexi forced out a short, breezy laugh. "Of course Quentin wanted to be with me. We've spent just about every New Year's Eve together for the past twenty years. Old habits die hard."

"Is that so?" Asha didn't sound convinced by the explanation.

Even Michael had a speculative gleam in his eyes as he divided a look between his two longtime friends.

Deliberately clearing her throat, Lexi glanced around the table and asked brightly, "What time are we leaving to go sightseeing?"

"Actually," Reese hedged, "we were just discussing that before you and Quentin came downstairs. Don't kill me, Lexi, but I'm not up for another day of sightseeing. Judging by my swollen ankles and sore back, I must have overdone it at the party last night."

Michael shook his head at Lexi. "I kept telling her to take it easy, but you know how stubborn she can be."

Lexi grinned sympathetically. "You know doctors make the worst patients. And since Reese is an obstetrician, she *definitely* thinks she knows best."

"That's because I do." Grinning unabashedly, Reese rubbed her bulging belly and continued, "Anyway, girl, my overprotective husband has sentenced me to a day of cozying in front of a fire and watching movies with him."

Lexi gave a mock shudder. "You poor woman."

"I know." Reese sighed dramatically. "But I'll survive."

Everyone laughed.

Turning her attention to Samara, Lexi asked hopefully, "What about you and Marcus?"

Samara grimaced. "I'm afraid we'll have to bail on you too. Dad and Marcus promised to take the boys fishing today, and somehow Mom and I got roped into joining them."

Lexi was aghast. "*Fishing?* In January?"

"Winter's the best season to go," asserted Sterling, an avid outdoorsman. "The lakes are less crowded, and I've caught some really big bass this time of year."

"If you say so, Dad," Lexi said skeptically.

Asha chuckled. "Believe me, *chère,* I'd much rather follow Michael and Reese's lead and spend the day lazing around a cozy fire. But a promise is a promise." Her lips curved. "So it looks as though you and Quentin are on your own until dinnertime."

"Looks that way," Lexi said weakly.

When she hazarded a glance at Quentin, he gave her the slow, lazy grin of a scoundrel. A grin she knew all too well.

As her pulse accelerated, she realized that for the first time ever, she was positively terrified to be alone with him.

So much for proving that nothing had changed between them.

Chapter 3

An hour later, Lexi and Quentin were ensconced in the backseat of a chauffeured car bound for Dijon, the capital of Burgundy and the birthplace of Dijon mustard.

The narrow, rambling roads meandered through a scenic countryside of gently rolling hills covered with dense forests and luscious vineyards that cascaded down sloping ridges. The glazed, multihued roof tiles of châteaus added vivid splashes of color to the landscape. It looked like something right out of a van Gogh painting.

"Oh, look!" Lexi said excitedly to Quentin, pointing to a herd of cattle grazing peacefully on a hillside.

Leaning over to peer out her window, Quentin cocked an amused brow at her. "Cows?"

"Not just *any* cows," she archly informed him. "Those are white Charolais cattle, which are specially bred to provide the superior quality of beef used in boeuf bourguignon, Burgundy's most well-known dish."

"Wait. Haven't you made that for me before?"

She smiled. "Several times."

Quentin gazed at the passing herd of cattle with newfound respect. "God bless each and every one of y'all."

When Lexi laughed, he grinned at her. And just like that, the awkwardness between them was gone. For good, Lexi hoped, though somehow she knew better.

Soon they arrived in Dijon, a gorgeous city characterized by historic buildings and cathedrals, art galleries and museums, upscale boutiques, antiques shops and medieval half-timbered houses nestled along cobbled streets. There were restaurants and cafés with terraces on every corner, offering gastronomic delights to please any palate.

Lexi took in the amazing sights, sounds and smells with the excited wonder of a child, tugging Quentin from one place to the next. The regal Palace of the Dukes of Burgundy was closed for the holiday, but they were able to explore the courtyards and climb up the Philippe le Bon Tower, which offered a wonderful view of Dijon and the surrounding countryside.

Next they visited the church of Notre Dame, an architecturally beautiful gothic building famous for the unusual gargoyles that covered its facade. There was an owl sculpted into one of the stone walls. In keeping with local custom, Lexi and Quentin took turns placing their left hands on the carving to make a wish.

As they started away, Quentin asked, "What'd you wish for?"

She smiled enigmatically. "If I tell you, it might not come true."

And that can't happen, she silently added. She hadn't wished for fame and fortune upon the release of her first cookbook next month. She hadn't even wished for a better relationship with her mother. Instead, she'd offered up a simple but heartfelt prayer that she and Quentin would always remain the best of friends. Because she couldn't bear the thought of ever losing him.

After stopping at a sidewalk café to enjoy a local favorite—kir, a white wine and cassis apéritif—they headed to an open-air market that specialized in breads, cheeses, wines, spices and sauces. Lexi had only intended to browse, but as they wandered through the bustling stalls, she found herself reaching for one item after another, her mind racing with ideas for different recipes.

Without being asked, Quentin retrieved a basket for her, a soft, indulgent smile quirking his lips as he watched her shop. "Don't forget what Asha said."

Mulling over a wedge of Epoisses cheese that she could serve with a bottle of Chablis, Lexi asked absently, "What'd she say?"

"You and Mike are her guests this weekend, so you're not allowed to step foot inside her kitchen to cook."

Lexi groaned. "It's so unfair. Asking a chef not to cook while in France is like asking a NASCAR driver to remain in neutral on the racetrack." She scowled. "Damn that woman."

Quentin laughed. "Tell you what, sweetness. If you don't want all these ingredients going to waste," he said, holding up the overflowing basket, "you can cook something for me when we get back home in two days."

Lexi brightened at once. "That's an *excellent* idea."

He grinned. "Just doing my part," he said gallantly, as if he were making the ultimate sacrifice by allowing her to prepare a meal for him. But the truth was that he loved her cooking as much as she loved cooking for him. Nothing pleased Lexi more than watching Quentin devour her food.

And the more praise he heaped on her, the more she wanted to cater to him.

After depositing the groceries in the chauffeured car, they decided to go for a quick wine tasting. Since Asha's sommelier had already promised to give everyone a guided tour of the château's cellars and vineyards tomorrow, Lexi and Quentin stopped by an indoor market operated by a local family of winemakers. The large tasting room lured passersby to venture inside to sample some of the region's finest pinot noirs and chardonnays.

The place was crowded with holiday tourists. After receiving glossy brochures and a breathless greeting from the harried young woman at the entrance, Lexi and Quentin were pretty much on their own.

At the first tasting table, Lexi showed Quentin the proper way to "nose" wine.

"To really appreciate the flavor of a wine," she explained, "you sniff it before tasting. The proper technique is to hold the stem of the glass, stick your nose into the bowl and let the scent rise up." As she demonstrated, she cautioned him, "Don't try to inhale the scent, or you'll mostly get alcohol fumes. Here, try it."

Of course Quentin inhaled, then gasped as the pungent fumes shot up his nose. He took a hasty gulp of wine that went down the wrong way and sent him into a violent coughing paroxysm.

Alarmed, Lexi took the glass from his hand, set it down and pounded him on the back as he wheezed and choked.

"Are you all right, sweetie?" she asked worriedly as several curious heads turned in their direction.

Quentin staggered back a step, his eyes rolling up in his head.

Lexi swept a panicked glance over the crowd. She was

about to call out for a doctor when she saw the mischievous grin on Quentin's face.

"Gotcha!"

Torn between relief and fury, Lexi punched him on the arm. "Idiot! I thought you were choking to death!"

He laughed. "From inhaling wine?"

She skewered him with a glare. "You play too damn much, Quentin."

As she turned and stalked out of the market, he caught her from behind, engulfing her as he draped his long arms around her shoulders and kissed the top of her head.

"Come on, Lex," he cajoled. "Don't be mad. I was just having some fun with you. I love it when you kick into professor mode. You're so serious and adorable."

"Don't call me adorable," Lexi grumbled darkly. "Not when I'm seriously contemplating how to kick your ass."

Quentin laughed, the deep, rumbling sound sending heat from the base of her skull to the bottom of her spine. Although his legs were much longer than hers, he effortlessly matched her stride, step for step. As though it were as natural to him as his own heartbeat.

"I'm sorry I scared you, Lex. I won't do it again, I promise."

She frowned. "One of these days you're going to push me too far, and I'm not going to forgive you."

"Don't say that."

"Why not?"

"Because you'd break my heart."

"It'd serve you right." But she was smiling now. She couldn't help it. He was downright irresistible when he said things like that to her. And he knew it.

"Hold up." He drew her to a stop. "Stay right there."

Puzzled, Lexi turned and watched as he sauntered over

to a street vendor selling flowers. He exchanged a few words with the woman in his adorably rudimentary French, which Lexi had been teaching him. When he flashed his killer grin, the vendor blushed and beamed at him.

Lexi sighed and rolled her eyes heavenward. *Another one bites the dust.*

A group of tourists strolled by, blocking her view of Quentin. She stood on tiptoe, wishing, not for the first time, that she were taller. Her height, topping out at five-two, had been the bane of her existence for as long as she could remember.

Which was why she hated supermodels.

Like Giselle.

Moments later Quentin reappeared, his arms tucked behind his back.

Lexi shook her head at him. "I don't care how pretty—"

He handed her a beautiful bouquet of fresh-cut flowers, and she gasped with shocked pleasure. Roses and anemones, from her favorite van Gogh print that he'd given her years ago!

"Oh, Quentin… Damn."

He smiled down at her. "Truce?"

She buried her nose in the fragrant flowers and sighed. "Truce."

His smile widened.

"You are very lucky woman!" the street vendor called out to Lexi.

"Merci beaucoup!" she called back, not bothering to correct the woman's assumption that she and Quentin were a couple.

Quentin glanced at his watch, then took her hand and started purposefully down the cobbled street.

"Where are we going?" Lexi asked curiously.

"We have an appointment."

"To do what?"

"You'll see."

Something in his enigmatic tone sent off warning bells in her head. She pulled up short, tugging her hand free of his. "I'm not taking another step until you tell me where we're going."

He scowled at her. "Damn, baby girl. Why can't you just go with the flow?"

"Quentin," she said warningly.

He heaved a short, frustrated breath. "I'm taking you on a hot-air balloon ride."

"What?" The blood drained from Lexi's head. "No way."

"Why not?"

"I don't want to."

"It'll be fun. Flying over the region, getting an aerial view."

She swallowed dryly. "It's too cold."

He gave her a knowing look. "We've been walking around for hours, and you haven't complained about the weather once."

"Yeah, but going thousands of feet into the air—"

"Ever heard of heat rising?"

"Actually, that's a myth. Nice try, though."

He groaned. "Come on, Lex. You can't visit Burgundy without taking a hot-air balloon ride."

"Why not? I'm sure plenty of other people do."

"They're not you," he countered. "The woman *I* know experiences life to the fullest. Always has."

She shook her head regretfully. "I can't, Quentin."

"Tell me why."

She exhaled a deep breath and met his direct gaze. "You know I'm afraid of heights."

"I know."

Of course he does. "So why are you pressuring me to do this?"

His gaze gentled, his hazel eyes plumbing the depths of hers. "You know I won't let anything happen to you."

She gave a grim, shaky laugh. "If the balloon malfunctioned, Q, there'd be nothing you could do about it."

"Do you trust me?"

She searched his solemn face and had the uncanny feeling that he was referring to more than the balloon ride.

"Of course I trust you," she said quietly. "You're my best friend."

"Then fly with me."

She stared at him for a prolonged moment, then swallowed hard and nodded, taking the plunge. "Okay," she whispered.

"You'll do it?"

"Yes." She shot him a surly glance. "But if something goes wrong and we plunge to our deaths, just know that my ghost will haunt yours for all eternity."

Quentin laughed, kissing her forehead. "I'll take my chances."

The ballooning company was located along the Burgundy Canal. The friendly, English-speaking pilot introduced himself, went over some housekeeping rules and explained their flight itinerary. And then, before Lexi could change her mind, they were boarding the hot-air balloon. The interior was divided into compartments that separated the pilot from the passengers, giving them a sense of privacy. The basket was lined with cushion and seemed sturdier than Lexi had feared.

But minutes later when the balloon lifted off, her stomach pitched sickeningly. She clung to Quentin, closing her eyes and burying her face in the cool, battered leather of his jacket. He wrapped his arms around her, gently stroking his hand up and down her back and whispering to her the way he might soothe a frightened child.

She could feel the balloon rising higher into the air, soaring toward the sky. Her heart galloped into her throat. A clammy sweat broke out over her skin and she shivered uncontrollably. Quentin opened his jacket and she shamelessly burrowed against his broad chest, taking refuge in the masculine heat and strength that enveloped her.

"You're going to be okay," Quentin murmured, brushing his lips against her temple. "Just take slow, deep breaths."

Lexi did as he told her. She hated this irrational fear of hers, hated that it made her so vulnerable. So pathetic.

She didn't know how much time passed. At some point the gripping panic receded, giving way to a sense of calm that made her feel stronger, more in control of herself.

"Lex," Quentin said softly. "Look what you're missing."

She cracked one eye open, then another.

Her breath escaped her in a soft gasp.

They were floating—*floating!*—over Burgundy.

A spectacular kaleidoscope of shapes and colors bombarded her at once. She could see every shade of green covering the slopes of the vineyards. The shiny roofs of châteaus and castles glistened under the late afternoon sun. Clusters of cottages and ancient stone churches were scattered across picturesque villages. The dark ribbon of a canal meandered lazily through forests. The lush beauty of the Saône river valley beckoned, and a rich palette of brown and gold identified the fields of Cote-d'Or.

Lexi stared out in rapt fascination. "Oh, my God, Quentin," she breathed. "This is… I'm speechless."

Quentin grinned down at her. "*That* doesn't happen very often."

"Very funny," she retorted, barely sparing him a glance. She was afraid the stunning vistas would disappear if she so much as blinked.

Keeping one arm securely around her waist, Quentin shifted so that they stood side by side.

Lexi raised her face to the azure sky, soaking up the sun and wind as the balloon glided smoothly through the air. It was absolutely exhilarating. A feast for the senses.

Over the next hour she and Quentin took in the sights, mostly communicating without words. When Lexi excitedly pointed something out to him, he'd nod and smile in shared appreciation. The pilot rarely interrupted to narrate, leaving his two passengers cocooned in their own private world of enjoyment.

When Quentin left her side, Lexi murmured softly, "Hurry back."

A moment later, she was startled by the sound of a bottle being uncorked.

Turning, she watched as Quentin poured champagne into two glasses and handed one to her. Surprised, she arched a brow at him. "I thought the champagne toast is traditionally done *after* the safe landing."

"I asked them to make an exception this time." A crooked grin curved his mouth. "I'd figured at some point during the flight, you'd appreciate some alcohol to help calm your nerves."

Lexi chuckled. "Good looking out."

"Always." Sobering after a moment, Quentin raised his glass in a toast to her, his eyes glowing with warm pride. "Here's to you. For bravely conquering your fear of heights."

Lexi smiled shyly. "I don't know if I've *completely* conquered it."

"You're up here, aren't you?"

Her smile turned quiet and grateful. "I couldn't have done it without you, Quentin."

His gaze softened. "We make a good team."

"Always."

Their glasses clinked musically and they drank, smiling at each other.

After a few moments, Lexi sighed contentedly. "What an amazing day this has been. I almost wish we didn't have to go back home on Monday."

"Me too," Quentin murmured.

"I'd love to have dinner tonight in one of those Michelin-rated French restaurants."

"Let's do it, then."

"We can't," she reminded him with a rueful smile. "Asha's chef is preparing a special New Year's Day dinner. Besides, we don't have reservations."

"Then we'll come back tomorrow night."

"Mmm. Sounds like a plan."

"Good." Quentin reached out, his fingertips brushing her cheek as he gently pushed her windswept hair off her face.

Their gazes caught and held. A strange, intoxicating dizziness swept through Lexi.

Altitude, she told herself. *Or too much wine in one day.*

But she knew better.

The winds of change were upon her and Quentin. That stolen kiss on the balcony had set something in motion between them. Something that had sent them hurtling into the unknown.

Where they landed, only time would tell.

Chapter 4

"How was your trip?"

Lexi jumped at the sound of her mother's voice, which had snapped her out of her deep reverie. She'd been daydreaming about Burgundy.

And Quentin.

Turning from the kitchen sink, where she'd just finished washing dishes, she saw her mother standing in the doorway, puffing on a cigarette. Carlene Austin had been on the phone when Lexi had arrived at the house half an hour ago. She'd greeted her daughter with a distracted wave and returned to her conversation while Lexi headed into the kitchen. At the sight of dirty dishes piled into the sink, she'd sighed in resignation, then rolled up her sleeves and gotten right to work. Old habits died hard.

Carlene shuffled into the small kitchen. "Thanks for taking care of that for me. The dishwasher's acting up again."

"I figured. Have you called someone?"

"No point. I can't afford the repairs." After thirty years in civil service, Carlene still complained of earning barely enough to make ends meet.

"It's just as well," Lexi said, twisting off the water faucet. "The dishwasher's old. No sense in sinking more money into it. We can go shopping to get you a new one this weekend."

"You buying?"

"Of course."

"Thanks, baby." Carlene sat down at the oak breakfast table, tapping her cigarette into an ashtray already bristling with butts. She'd once been beautiful, with a smooth caramel complexion and long, glossy black hair that she'd meticulously maintained. But time and bitterness, compounded with an unhealthy nicotine habit, had taken their toll. Now there was a hard edge to her features, dark circles rimmed her eyes, her hair and skin had lost their sheen, and the shapely figure she'd once flaunted had withered away to the gaunt frame now swallowed up in a chenille robe.

Averting her troubled gaze, Lexi vigorously wiped down the countertops. She could see through the alcove into the living room that the heavy curtains were drawn closed, plunging the room into gloomy darkness. The worn, outdated furniture reeked of every cigarette Carlene had ever smoked. The whole house did.

Shaking off the depressing thought, Lexi dropped the dishrag into the sink and joined her mother at the table.

"When do you go back to work?" Carlene asked.

"Tomorrow." A chef instructor at Le Cordon Bleu College of Culinary Arts, Lexi couldn't wait to tell her students all about her trip to Burgundy.

Carlene drew on her cigarette and shot twin streams

of smoke through her nostrils. "You gonna keep working after your cookbook comes out?"

"Of course. You know I love teaching."

Her mother grunted noncommittally. The idea of enjoying one's livelihood was a foreign concept to her. She'd never reaped personal fulfillment from her government job. It had been a means to an end, a way to feed and clothe her three young children after her philandering husband had walked out on them. His desertion, followed by a string of failed relationships over the years, had turned Carlene into a miserable, embittered woman.

As Lexi stared at the glowing red tip of her mother's cigarette, she had a flashback to the time when she was fourteen and Carlene had burst into her bedroom late one night, screaming at the top of her lungs because Lexi had forgotten to wash the dishes before going to bed. Trailing cigarette ashes, Carlene had stormed across the room and snatched the covers off her daughter's body, cursing at her to get up. Shaken and disoriented, Lexi hadn't moved fast enough. The next thing she knew, her mother was leaning over her and viciously stabbing the butt of her cigarette into Lexi's thigh. The searing, excruciating pain had wrenched an agonized wail from her that brought her two younger siblings running from their bedroom.

The sound of their confused, frightened sobs had penetrated Carlene's black rage. Her horrified gaze had swept over Lexi, writhing in pain on the floor. As the enormity of what she'd done sank in, Carlene had backed out of the room and fled from the apartment, leaving Lexi behind to console her distraught siblings before she could tend to her own wound.

The next morning, it was a humble, contrite Carlene who'd entered her daughter's bedroom carrying a breakfast tray. Lexi had lain there, silent and unmoving, as her mother gently applied a salve to her burn and dressed it with gauze, assuring her that the scar would eventually fade. It had, but the memory of that harrowing night had lingered for years, as raw and painful as ever.

As Lexi watched now, ashes crumbled off the butt of her mother's cigarette and landed on the table. Carlene didn't seem to notice or care.

Frowning, Lexi got up to retrieve the dishrag. Returning to the table, she wiped away the ashes, wishing she could erase her memories just as easily.

"I thought you were trying to quit," she told her mother.

"Don't start with me," Carlene warned. "I don't need no damn lecture from you."

"I wasn't going to lecture you." Lexi silently counted to ten. "However, you really *do* need to take better care of yourself, Ma. Your doctor's right. You're playing Russian roulette with your life by smoking the way you do."

Carlene took a long, defiant drag on her cigarette and blew a cloud of smoke right into Lexi's face. Though her eyes stung, she refused to flinch. She wouldn't give her mother the satisfaction.

The strategy worked.

Scowling, Carlene stubbed out her cigarette with short, angry jabs punctuated with muttered expletives. "I'm getting sick and tired of you telling me what to do in my own goddamn house."

Technically, the house belonged as much to Lexi as it did to Carlene. She'd helped her mother purchase the property by cosigning the mortgage loan and supplying the closing funds. If her cookbook sold well—and by all early indications it would—she intended to buy her mother some badly needed new furniture, which she'd been unable to do at the time because she'd nearly depleted her savings account.

"You never answered my question," Carlene said sourly. "How was Paris?"

"It was great," Lexi replied. "But we didn't actually stay in Paris. Asha has an amazing château in the countryside."

"A château?" Carlene's voice dripped with scorn. "Well, well, well. Look at you, Miss Thang. Moving up in the world."

Lexi tensed, mentally kicking herself for forgetting one of her cardinal rules: *Always downplay your good fortune to avoid rubbing salt into the wound of your mother's broken dreams.*

"I have something for you." Hoping to placate Carlene, Lexi reached inside a bag under the table and withdrew one of the bottles of wine she'd brought back from Burgundy.

Carlene took the bottle, her dark eyes narrowing on the gold leaf label.

"Pinot noir," Lexi volunteered. "It's a red wine. Very rich."

"I bet. It looks expensive. How much did it cost?"

"I meant rich in flavor. Full-bodied. And it didn't cost me anything." Lexi hesitated. "It's a gift from Asha. From her vineyard."

She half expected her mother to hurl the bottle across the room. Instead Carlene arched a surprised brow. "She grows wine, too? On top of running a fashion company? Good Lord, what *doesn't* that woman have her hands all over?"

Lexi shrugged. "She considers herself a connoisseur. Er, she enjoys good wine," she quickly amended, lest she be accused of throwing around fancy words. "When she bought the château several years ago, she didn't want the surrounding vineyards to go to waste. So she decided to go into the winemaking business. But she's pretty much hands-off. Her employees run the whole operation."

"While *she* gets richer," Carlene said, her voice laced with jealousy. "Must be nice."

Lexi said nothing. She would *not* be baited into a petty argument over Asha Dubois. God knows she and her mother had quarreled enough when she'd told her that she was spending New Year's at Asha's second home in France. Carlene had accused her of preferring the company of strangers over her own family, even though Lexi had just spent Christmas with her—unlike her brother and sister, who'd wisely opted to stay in New York for the holidays.

How many times had Lexi questioned her sanity for remaining in Atlanta all these years? After graduating from the French Culinary Institute in New York, she could have easily justified putting down roots there. But she'd come back home, compelled by forces she couldn't explain. Her siblings called her a glutton for punishment. Maybe they were right.

"Thanks for the wine," Carlene said. "I'm sure I'll enjoy it."

Encouraged by the uncharacteristically gracious words, Lexi smiled. "Maybe you and I could go there together next time."

"Where? To France?" Her mother snorted. "Why would I wanna go there? They hate Americans."

"Not all of them. I met some very warm, friendly French people."

"Sorry, baby. Not interested."

Of course, Lexi mused. What was she thinking? Her mother had never stepped foot outside of Georgia, let alone traveled to another country.

"How's Michael doing?" Carlene asked.

"Great. He and Reese are so excited about the baby. They've got the nursery set up in their new house, and they've been eagerly counting down to the due date."

"That's nice." Carlene heaved a lamenting sigh. "Shame you couldn't snatch him up before *she* did. All those years of friendship. Seems like such a waste."

Here we go again, Lexi thought with a sigh. She and her mother had covered this territory so many times, she already knew what was coming next.

"Maybe if you hadn't spent so much time trying to be one of the boys, Michael would have seen you more as a woman he could love."

Striving for patience, Lexi said evenly, "I know this is still hard for you to believe, Ma, but I've never been romantically interested in Michael. And I'm glad he never saw me as more than just a friend. He and Reese are absolutely perfect for each other. I'm happy for them, and I wish you could be, too."

Carlene sniffed disdainfully. "I never said I wasn't happy for them. I'm just pointing out that you've known Michael longer than Reese has. So if anyone should have clipped his bachelor wings, it should've been you."

Lexi shook her head at her mother's warped logic. "I've been friends with Quentin just as long," she challenged, "and I don't hear you saying the same thing about *him*."

"Quentin?" Carlene scoffed with a laugh. "Oh, baby, that one's a lost cause. A rascal through and through. Even his own mama knows he's never going to settle down and give her grandbabies."

"Things change," Lexi heard herself saying. "People change."

Her mother snorted. "Not Quentin Reddick. Even if you *were* his type—"

Lexi bristled. "Quentin doesn't have a 'type.' He's an equal-opportunity womanizer."

Carlene's brows shot up. "Why are you getting so huffy? It's not like *you're* interested in Quentin."

"Of course not," Lexi snapped irritably. "But when you say things like that to me, you make me feel like I'm not even attractive enough to catch the eye of someone like Quentin."

"Of course you are. But all the good looks in the world can't keep a man who's hardwired to stray." A nasty, satisfied gleam lit Carlene's eyes. "You know that as well as I do."

Lexi flinched as the verbal dagger struck home. She should have been immune by now to her mother's penchant for cruelty, but she wasn't. After years of railing bitterly against unfaithful men, Carlene had felt vindicated when Lexi caught her husband cheating on her. Since the divorce, Carlene had never missed an opportunity to remind her daughter that they were more alike than Lexi wanted to believe.

"Just once," she said in a low, strained voice, "could you at least *pretend* to be sorry that my marriage only lasted two years?"

Carlene sputtered, taking umbrage. "Why would you say something like that to me? I *did* feel bad for you!"

"You sure have a funny way of showing it."

"Don't put this back on me," her mother snapped. "I *told* you Adam McNamara was no good, but you insisted on marrying him anyway! If you'd just listened—"

Lexi threw up a trembling hand. "Can we not talk about this tonight? It's bad enough that the date of my wedding anniversary is coming up next week."

Carlene faltered, something like pity softening her features. "I forgot."

Lexi's mouth twisted sardonically. "I wish I could."

In the ensuing silence, her mother removed a pack of Newport cigarettes from the pocket of her robe. She toyed with it for a moment, then reluctantly set it aside. In a more conciliatory tone, she said to Lexi, "You haven't finished telling me about your trip."

Lexi hesitated, then admitted, "It was wonderful."

"Really? What was so wonderful about it?"

"Everything. The food, the wine, the scenery." She smiled faintly. "The balloon ride was definitely one of the highlights."

"Come again?"

At her mother's dumbfounded look, Lexi laughed. "Quentin convinced me to go on a hot-air balloon ride with him. Can you believe it? *Me,* the woman who's so afraid of heights I have to take sedatives before getting on a plane. Shocking, right?"

"Not that shocking," Carlene drawled in amusement. "That rascal can talk a woman into doing anything—and probably has."

Lexi smiled distractedly. For the first time in days, she had something other than Quentin's powers of persuasion on her mind. "You know, Ma, I've always wondered why I'm so terrified of heights."

Carlene hesitated. "Some people have phobias. That's always been yours."

"I know. But it's so damn *paralyzing.* It's almost like...I don't know. It's hard to explain."

There was a small silence.

Carlene was suddenly eyeing her pack of cigarettes like a junkie craving a fix.

Lexi smiled wryly. "If I didn't know better, I would think something happened to me when I was a baby. Maybe one of the nurses dropped me, or—"

Her mother's gaze swung sharply to hers. "Or what? What are you asking me?"

Taken aback by her reaction, Lexi stammered, "N-nothing. I'm just—"

"What the hell's gotten into you tonight? First you accuse me of not being sympathetic enough about your divorce. Now you're accusing me of, what, child abuse?"

Lexi frowned. "Of course not."

"You've never forgiven me for what happened that night," Carlene fumed bitterly. "No matter how many times I've apologized for what I did, you're still holding it against me!"

"That's not true!" Lexi burst out in angry disbelief. "If I still blamed you, would I be here? You treat me like crap, Ma, but guess what? I'm. Still. *Here*."

Resentment darkened her mother's face. "I know what this is about. You spent the weekend with that bourgeois woman and decided she was a better mother than me because she's rich and sophisticated and drinks fine wine. Well, let me tell you something. I did everything for you and your siblings when you were growing up. *Everything!* I have nothing to—"

Lexi shoved her chair back from the table and stood on trembling legs. She'd had enough of her mother's diatribes for one night. "I can't do this. I need to go."

Carlene said nothing as she stalked out of the room to retrieve her coat from the hall closet. She jammed her arms into the sleeves, struggling to get her emotions under control before she got behind the wheel to drive home.

When it became apparent that her mother wasn't going to see her to the door or even say good night, she sighed harshly and strode back into the kitchen.

Carlene was already lighting up another cigarette.

"Good night, Ma," Lexi said tersely.

Sucking in a lungful of smoke, her mother gave her a dismissive wave. The same way she'd greeted her when she arrived.

As Lexi slammed out of the house, she wondered, for the millionth time, what the hell was keeping her in Atlanta.

Chapter 5

On the other side of town, Quentin sat alone at the end of a long mahogany bar in Wolf's Soul, a popular Atlanta restaurant owned by his best friend, Michael. Quentin was hunched over a bottle of beer he'd been nursing for the past half hour.

Taking a long sip, he looked up at the plasma television mounted above the counter. A rerun of Michael's Emmy-winning show, *Howlin' Good,* was on the air. It was one of the "macho man" themed episodes, which featured no-frills recipes geared toward "manly" appetites. Michael hosted one of these shows every season as an opportunity to invite his father's old police comrades to fill the studio audience. The men stomped, hollered and cheered their way through the whole taping. And viewers loved every rowdy minute of it.

Quentin watched in brooding silence, his eyes glazing over the familiar images.

"Whose funeral was today?"

He glanced around as Michael plopped down on the stool beside him, dressed in his white chef's jacket and black pants.

"What's up, man?" he greeted Quentin, clapping him on the back.

Quentin grunted in response.

A bottle of beer materialized before Michael. "On the house, boss," the bartender said with a wink and a grin.

Michael grinned back, raising his bottle in a mock toast.

The man hitched his chin toward Quentin. "Can I get you another cold one, Counselor?"

"Naw, I'm good. Thanks."

As the bartender moved off to tend to another customer, Michael took a swig of beer and eyed Quentin's brooding profile. "Seriously, man. Did someone die?"

"No," Quentin murmured. "I just have a lot on my mind."

"Of course." Michael nodded. "The trial starts tomorrow. That's all Marcus has been talking about for weeks."

Last year, Marcus Wolf's prominent law firm had been renamed Wolf & Reddick, LLP to reflect Quentin's changed status as joint owner. One of his first moves had been to file a lawsuit on behalf of an employee who'd been wrongfully terminated by a health-insurance company after he spoke out against his employer's fraudulent claim-denial practices. As lead counsel, Quentin would argue the case before the Georgia Court of Appeals.

The upcoming trial should have been uppermost on his mind tonight. The pure adrenaline rush of preparing for a big case, the anticipation of going up against a formidable adversary. *This* was what he lived for.

So why were his thoughts dominated by a woman he couldn't have—and had no business wanting?

Michael was talking, his deep voice blending into the other background noise that filled the busy restaurant. "...says you're the best litigator to take on those health-insurance sharks. He says you've been salivating at the opportunity to make mincemeat of them in court."

Quentin took a long pull on his beer, humming the appropriate "mmm-hmm" to let Michael know he was listening. Even though he wasn't.

There was a pause.

"On second thought," Michael continued, "what Marcus *really* said is that you're gonna totally blow the case. He thinks you're gonna be outmatched and outmaneuvered by the defense team's high-powered lawyers."

"Uh-huh," Quentin murmured, his mind drifting thousands of miles away to Burgundy, and the balloon ride with Lexi. He remembered the way she'd gazed out across the stunning landscape, her face aglow with wonder and exhilaration. After a while, he'd found himself watching her more than the view. Because as amazing as the sights were, he knew the experience wouldn't have been the same without her by his side.

"...planning a surprise baby shower. And Lexi says she's going to—"

Quentin swung his head around to stare at Michael. "What'd you say?"

A knowing gleam filled his friend's eyes. "So *that's* what it took to finally get your attention. Hearing Lexi's name."

Quentin frowned and glanced away, sipping his beer. But he could feel Michael studying him, his eyes shrewd and assessing. He instinctively braced himself for the question he knew was coming.

"What's going on between you and Lexi?"

"Nothing," Quentin lied without missing a beat.

"Bull. I saw the way you two were acting around each other this past weekend. There were all *kinds* of vibes jumping off both of you. And what about all that stuff Asha was saying over breakfast? Sounded to me like she was on to something."

Quentin said nothing, absently rubbing his thumb back and forth against the frosty condensation lining his beer bottle. He and Michael had been best friends since childhood. Next to Lexi, no one knew Quentin better than Michael. Which meant he knew the good *and* the bad. Unfortunately, when it came to Quentin's track record with women, there was more bad than good.

Michael blew out a long, deep breath. "Look, Q, you know nothing would please me more than to see my two best friends happy. It'd be weird as hell if you and Lexi hooked up after all these years," he admitted with a rueful grin, "but I'd be totally cool with it—as long as both of you were committed to making the relationship work."

Quentin knew *he* was the only one whose commitment issues were in question.

"The last thing I want is for Lexi to get hurt again," Michael said quietly. "We both know how much she went through with that cheating bastard she was married to."

Quentin clenched his jaw, his fingers tightening around the neck of his beer bottle at the reminder of Adam McNamara. The worthless son of a bitch had done a number on Lexi, leaving her heartbroken and more disillusioned about men than she'd already been. Two years later, Quentin was still out for McNamara's blood. The only reason he hadn't killed the bastard was that Lexi had vowed she'd never visit him in prison, and he didn't want to call her bluff. He'd promised her that he wouldn't go after her ex-husband, and he intended to keep his word. But if he ever ran into McNamara in a dark, deserted alley, all bets were off.

"He never deserved her," Quentin growled with renewed fury.

"Not by a long shot," Michael agreed grimly. "Anyway, after everything she's been through, she needs someone who's reliable. Someone she can trust, someone she doesn't have to check up on every hour of the day to make sure he ain't creepin'. She needs someone who's ready to commit to one woman."

Quentin smiled cynically. "And you think that someone can't be me. Because I can't change my ways."

Michael pinned him with a direct gaze. "*You* tell *me*."

They stared each other down, the air between them fraught with challenge.

Michael was the first to break eye contact, his gaze skipping past Quentin to stare across the crowded restaurant. By the way his expression softened, Quentin didn't have to guess who'd just walked through the door.

He glanced over his shoulder. Sure enough, Reese was heading straight toward them, her round belly protruding through her open lab coat, a stethoscope dangling around her neck. Customers called out friendly greetings to her, and she responded in kind.

As she reached the bar, she said warmly, "Hey, fellas."

"Hey, baby girl," Quentin said.

"Hiya, sweetheart." Swiveling around on his stool, Michael tugged gently on her stethoscope and pulled her close for an affectionate kiss. "You forgot to remove this. Busy day?"

"Very. Delivered eight babies, including a set of twins." She smiled, looping her arms around his neck. "How was *your* day?"

"Good. Even better now that you're here."

Quentin rolled his eyes.

Catching his expression, Reese grinned at her husband. "I think we're grossing out our friend here."

"I know. Isn't it fun?"

"Absolutely."

They traded diabolical grins that coaxed a low chuckle out of Quentin.

"Are you hungry?" Michael asked Reese.

"Aren't I always?"

He smiled. "Let me fix you a plate, get you off your feet."

"No. Sit," she said as he started to rise. "I'm not an invalid. I can find my way to the kitchen. You boys finish your talk."

"Naw," Quentin drawled, "take your man with you. He's disturbing my meditation."

"Meditating?" Reese swept an amused glance around the crowded restaurant. "Here?"

"See, that's the beauty of meditation. You can do it anywhere." Quentin grinned wickedly. "Not unlike—"

Michael scowled. "Baby, why don't you head on back to the kitchen? I'll be there in a minute."

Reese laughed, wagging her finger at Quentin before waddling off.

Michael transferred his gaze to Quentin. "So we're straight, right?"

"About Lexi?"

Michael nodded. "If you're ready to be that someone, then make your move. But if you hurt her, I'm gonna have to kick your ass." He flashed a quick, sharp-edged smile that left no doubt in Quentin's mind that he'd make good on his threat. And then he was gone, easily catching up to his wife.

Quentin frowned after him, even as he grudgingly admitted to himself that Michael had every reason to question his intentions toward Lexi.

"Excuse me, handsome. Is this seat taken?"

Quentin glanced over his shoulder.

A woman stood right behind him.

Out of habit he looked her over, swiftly cataloging her assets. Slender and attractive, light-skinned with long hair and a pretty smile. Nice.

But she wasn't petite, he noted. And she wasn't curvy enough. She didn't have gypsy eyes that a man could drown in. Or a lush mouth made for sin. And her voice wasn't a soft rasp, laced with a lazy Southern drawl that made her sound like she'd been napping in the sun. Quentin knew that if this woman ever called him "sweetie," it wouldn't have the same effect on him.

Because she wasn't Lexi.

Lexi.

He got abruptly to his feet.

The woman stared at him as he peeled off some large bills from his wallet and dropped them onto the counter. "Drinks are on me, beautiful."

"Are you leaving?" she asked, sounding disappointed.

"Yes, ma'am."

"Alone?"

Quentin smiled to soften his rejection. "Alone."

But he wouldn't stay that way for very long.

Chapter 6

The first thing Lexi did when she got home was hop into the shower. She always left her mother's house smelling like an ashtray, and she hated it. Standing under the hot spray, she scrubbed her skin and vigorously shampooed her hair until she was squeaky clean.

When she emerged from the shower, she slipped on a pair of clean underwear and grabbed her blow-dryer. She'd just finished drying her hair when she was startled by a knock on the bathroom door.

"Lex," called a deep, masculine voice.

She whirled around, staring at the closed door. "Quentin?"

He chuckled. "Unless you've got a bunch of other guys running around with a spare key to your house." He paused. "You don't, do you?"

"I don't know." A smile tipped one corner of her mouth. "I can't remember."

Another pause. "That's not funny, Lex."

She laughed, secretly relieved that she always closed the bathroom door to keep steam trapped inside the room. The thought of Quentin spying on her while she took a shower brought a hot, embarrassed flush to her body. Not that he'd ever invade her privacy like that, of course. She'd gotten undressed in the same room with him many times, and he'd always kept his back turned like a perfect gentleman. But then again, he saw more than enough pairs of breasts on a regular basis. He didn't have to resort to sneaking a peek at his best friend's.

"What're you doing here, anyway?" Lexi called through the door as she returned her blow-dryer to the linen cabinet and removed a jar of mango body butter. "Shouldn't you be at the office burning the midnight oil in preparation for the trial?"

"Been doing that for the past five months," Quentin answered. "I need a break."

"Slacker," she teased.

He chuckled softly. "I just came from the restaurant."

Lexi didn't have to ask which restaurant. Not a week went by without one or both of them eating at Wolf's Soul. It was their favorite hangout, and the food was second to none.

"How long have you been here?"

"Not long. I rang the doorbell once or twice. When you didn't answer, I figured you were in the bathroom. So I just let myself in."

"No problem, sweetie." She began smoothing on the rich, scented body butter. First one arm, and then the other.

"You almost finished in there?"

"Almost. Just putting on some cream."

"Oh." Quentin's voice sounded strange, rough. "You're not, ah, dressed yet?"

"Not quite." She hesitated. "I had to blow-dry my hair. The heat makes me sweat, so I prefer to get dressed afterward." She grimaced, wondering why she'd volunteered so much information.

Quentin said nothing.

Bracing one foot on the edge of the bathtub, Lexi spread the fragrant cream over her thigh. She massaged it into her skin, working downward to her feet before moving to the other leg.

"I brought you something to eat," Quentin told her in that strangely thick tone.

She smiled. "Really? That was very thoughtful of you."

"I figured you probably hadn't eaten dinner yet."

"You figured correctly. As usual." Was she imagining things, or had his voice gotten closer to the door?

She swallowed, licking her lips. Staring at herself in the mirror, she began rubbing the mango butter over her belly. Her muscles quivered, tightened. She paused, then slowly slid her hands up to her breasts. An odd, tingling awareness rippled over her skin.

Without warning, her mind conjured an image of the doorknob being turned. A moment later Quentin stood in the doorway, his lids at half mast over smoldering hazel eyes. Their gazes locked in the mirror.

Without a word he started toward her, a slow, stealthy advance that made her pulse hammer.

When he'd reached the sink where she stood, he dipped his fingers into the jar of cream, scooping out enough to coat both of his hands. Her body hummed with arousal. He moved behind her, staring at their joined reflections in the mirror. A slow, sensual smile curved his mouth. And then he cupped her breasts.

Lexi gasped with pleasure.

He began to massage the cream into her breasts with a circular motion, starting from the outside and deliberately working his way toward her dark, distended nipples. He brushed his thumbs against them, gently rubbing and circling the areolae. Jolts of sensation raced to her groin. Her thighs shook, and her clitoris pulsed.

Quentin kneaded and caressed her breasts until they glistened and her eyes were glazed with desire. As his warm lips nuzzled the side of her throat, one hand began to slide down the front of her body. Her heart thundered. She trembled with anticipation, ached with need. And then his fingers were slipping beneath the waistband of her panties and touching—

"Lex? You okay in there?"

The sound of Quentin's voice snapped Lexi out of her erotic trance.

She stared in wide-eyed shock at her reflection in the mirror. At the sight of her sharply thrusting nipples, she gasped and flung her arms across her breasts. As if she could hide the evidence of her arousal from herself.

"Lex?" Quentin prompted again.

"I—I'm fine." Her voice was shaky.

"Are you sure? You made a noise. Like you were in pain."

Oh, God, she thought, cheeks flaming with mortification. Had she actually moaned *out loud?*

"I, uh, dropped something on my foot. But I'm fine. Really."

After a prolonged moment of silence, Quentin said gruffly, "I'll let you get dressed."

Yes! Please go away! "I'll be out in a few minutes."

"Okay."

When he'd gone, she let out a deep, shuddering breath

and leaned weakly against the sink, her hands braced on the counter for support.

What the hell was she doing? Having erotic fantasies about Quentin? *Quentin?* He was her best friend, for goodness' sake! Her confidant. The absolute *last* man on earth she should ever be lusting after. Yet that was exactly what she was doing. The steamy daydream had seemed so real, so shockingly explicit, that she'd been on the verge of climaxing before Quentin interrupted her.

Lexi groaned, bending over the sink to splash cold water on her flushed face. This was all *his* damn fault. Him and that scorching New Year's Eve kiss that had awakened all sorts of feelings and desires she'd never known existed. If he hadn't acted on a reckless impulse and kissed her that night, she wouldn't be standing here now—breathless and weak-kneed, with painfully erect nipples and a throbbing clitoris. And that was just from a fantasy! How much worse off would she be if he'd actually been inside the bathroom, doing those wickedly delicious things to her? If he'd actually made love to her?

A deep shudder swept through her. *Don't even go there,* she ordered herself. *You and Quentin Reddick will not be doing the horizontal tango. Not in this lifetime!*

No matter how sexy Quentin was—*and man, was he ever*—she couldn't allow herself to become romantically involved with him. If one stolen kiss could wreak such havoc on their friendship, making love would irrevocably alter the course of their lives. And considering that she'd spent the past two years trying to rebuild her life, the last thing Lexi needed was more emotional upheaval.

Dragging in a deep breath, she tugged on an old Spelman T-shirt and black leggings.

When she'd finished dressing, she surveyed her reflection in the bathroom mirror. As part of her postdivorce makeover, she'd had her hair cut into a short bob with longish bangs that swooped over one eye. It was chic, sleek and sexy, and the many compliments she'd received had given her a nice ego boost—something she'd needed desperately after Adam's humiliating betrayal. The best part about the bob was that she could wear it straight and it still looked good. So she didn't have to worry about curling her hair now to look presentable for Quentin. Besides, he'd seen her wearing big rollers on her head, ugly flannel pajamas and a cucumber mask on her face. Why let vanity get in the way now?

Sufficiently satisfied that she'd wrestled her rampant hormones into submission, Lexi left her bedroom and went in search of Quentin.

She found him in the kitchen, standing at the microwave built into the mahogany paneled cabinets. He'd shed his dark suit jacket and tie, tossing both over the back of a chair at the breakfast table. His white broadcloth shirt was untucked from his pants, the sleeves rolled up to strong forearms dusted with black hair. Lexi stared at the way his wide, muscular shoulders tapered down to narrow hips and those endlessly long legs.

Her mouth went dry. Had he always radiated such raw masculine energy? Such sex appeal? If so, how in the world had she remained immune all these years?

At that moment he glanced over his shoulder—and stared at her with an arrested expression on his face.

Pulse thudding, Lexi shifted self-consciously from one foot to another. "What's wrong?"

"Nothing." His lazy gaze ran the length of her. "That shirt you're wearing. It gave me flashbacks to college."

Except in college, I didn't fantasize about you stealing into my bathroom and running your hands all over my naked body.

Heat suffused her face.

Striving to maintain composure, she wandered into the kitchen, her bare feet padding across smooth hardwood. The mouthwatering aroma of braised baby back ribs wafted from the microwave. "Mmm, that smells good."

As she brushed past Quentin, he sniffed appreciatively at her. "*You* smell good."

"What—as opposed to the way I normally do?" Lexi quipped.

He grinned, playfully tweaking her nose. It was something he'd done a thousand times before. But now, even the simplest touch sent shivers up and down her spine.

Fighting to ignore her body's traitorous reaction to him, Lexi walked over to the gleaming Sub-Zero refrigerator and pulled one side open. "What's your poison?"

"Water's good, actually."

She grabbed two bottles of Perrier.

As she handed one to Quentin, he made a face. "Don't you ever have any *real* water?"

"Nope. Want real water?" She grinned, pointing to the sink faucet. "Knock yourself out."

"Damn, Lex, that's cold."

She laughed, hopping onto the granite countertop. "That's what you get for complaining about my Perrier, you ingrate."

"Keep talking and I'll eat all these ribs by myself. And you know I can."

"Don't you dare!"

He laughed, removing their hot food from the microwave. He passed her a plate, then lowered himself onto the long center island so that they were facing each other.

Lexi bit into a juicy rib, closed her eyes and groaned.

"Mmm. How'd you know I was in the mood for barbecue?"

Quentin gave her a lazy smile. "Don't you know by now that I can read your mind?"

She grinned weakly. "Of course. How could I forget?" *Thank God you really can't!*

"How was your day?" They spoke at the same time, then laughed softly.

Quentin said, "Do you realize we ask each other that question every day?"

"We do?" At his nod, Lexi shrugged. "So? What's wrong with that?"

"Nothing. It's just that…Mike and Reese…" Trailing off, he shook his head with a low chuckle. "Forget it. It's nothing."

Lexi ate a forkful of bourbon baked beans. "So how *was* your day?"

"Busy. Productive."

"I bet. Big day tomorrow." She grinned at him. "How's your adrenaline? Through the roof yet?"

"Not quite."

"Really?" That gave her pause. "Well, give it a few more hours, and you'll be bouncing off the walls."

"Probably." His answering smile was distracted. "How was *your* day?"

"Good. Samara and I had a conference call with Reese's sister, Raina, to finalize the plans for Reese's baby shower next Saturday. We really wanted to have it in Sterling's garden, but it's going to be too cold. So we're having it at the restaurant. Wait till you see how we decorate the place. It's going to be so beautiful."

"Yeah?" Quentin murmured, chewing his food.

Lexi grinned wryly. "Wait, what am I thinking? You don't care about decorations. You probably won't even notice them 'cause you'll be too busy flirting with all the single women there."

"Of course," Quentin drawled. "That's what I do."

Hearing the note of sarcasm in his voice, she arched a brow. "That *is* what you do."

"You never know," he said mildly. "I just might surprise you and keep to myself at the party."

"You?" As Lexi started to laugh, he pinned her with a look that instantly shut her up.

Ducking her head over her plate, she reached for another rib.

They ate in silence for a few minutes.

It was Quentin who spoke first. "What else did you do today?"

"Not much." Lexi hesitated. "I went to see Mom."

"Yeah?" His expression softened. "How'd that go?"

She shrugged. "It went."

Quentin frowned. He knew all too well about her tumultuous relationship with her mother, knew about the physical and emotional scars she bore. "Are you okay?"

"I'm fine." She forced a bright smile. "She really appreciated the bottle of wine."

Quentin gave her a skeptical look.

"She did," Lexi insisted. "She thanked me, said she'd enjoy it."

"Okay." Quentin searched her face, his eyes gentle and discerning. "What'd you argue about?"

"The usual." A smile of bitter irony touched her mouth. "If nothing else, Mom's consistent."

Quentin's jaw clenched. He'd always wanted to protect her from her mother, and it bothered him that he couldn't.

"I probably shouldn't have gone to see her so soon after

getting back," Lexi murmured ruefully. "I should have allowed the glow from Burgundy to wear off first."

"Mine definitely hasn't," Quentin said quietly.

They traded soft smiles.

After another moment, Lexi sighed. "I've been thinking."

Quentin set his empty plate down. "About?"

"How small my world is. How limited my experiences have become in recent years."

"What're you talking about?"

"I'm a professional chef, and I'd never even been to Burgundy."

"You've been to other parts of France," Quentin pointed out, wiping his hands on a napkin. "Not to mention several other countries. You're one of the most well traveled people I know, Lex."

"Maybe." She released a deep breath. "I guess what I'm trying to say is that I'm starting to feel restless. Like my life has settled into a routine."

Quentin looked bemused. "You signed a six-figure book deal two years ago. Your first cookbook hits the shelves next month. A whole new world's about to open up for you."

At that, Lexi broke into a chorus of "A Whole New World" from the animated movie *Aladdin*. "Come on, Red," she teasingly cajoled Quentin by invoking her affectionate nickname for him—"Red" being short for Reddick. "You sing Peabo Bryson's part."

"I don't think so." Quentin chuckled, taking a swig of water.

She grinned at him. "Do you know that song was playing in my head during our balloon ride?"

"Really?" Quentin paused to consider the lyrics, which she'd forced him to memorize years ago after they saw the movie together—also against his will. "I can see that. It fits."

"Perfectly."

They smiled at each other.

Sobering after another moment, Lexi said, "What I've been trying to get at is that I need a change of scenery."

Quentin's eyes narrowed. "What do you mean?"

She sighed. "I think it may be time for me to leave Atlanta."

Quentin went still. "Leave…Atlanta?"

She nodded slowly. "Don't get me wrong. I *love* the A-T-L. It's my home, always will be. But there are a lot of painful memories here for me. Everywhere I look, I see reminders of demons I need to exorcise. Even this house feels like a prison sometimes," she admitted, casting a troubled glance around the large gourmet kitchen. It was her favorite room in the house she'd once shared with her ex-husband, a sales executive she'd met at a nightclub several years ago.

Quentin frowned darkly. "I've told you to move, but you refuse."

"I know. And you're probably right. I *should* move. But I used to love this house, and I keep telling myself that if I'm patient, I'll feel that way again someday." She smiled wanly. "If only starting over were as simple as getting a new haircut and replacing my marriage bed."

Something inscrutable flickered in Quentin's eyes before he glanced down, absently peeling the label off his water bottle. "If you left Atlanta," he said in a low voice, "where would you go?"

"I don't know." Setting aside her empty plate, Lexi drew her knees up to her chest. "Colby and Summer have been begging me to join them in New York for years. They share an apartment, but they said we could get a bigger one if I moved in with them." She shrugged. "It might be fun to live under the same roof as my siblings again."

"What about your job?"

"There are other Le Cordon Bleu schools around the country, so I could easily transfer to any one of them. Honestly, with my credentials, I could teach just about anywhere." She paused. "Maybe even France."

Quentin's head snapped up. *"France?"*

"Sure, why not? I went to a French culinary school. I love the food, speak the language." She smiled. "Maybe I'd move to Burgundy and open my own café, something cozy where I could work on my cookbooks when it's not busy. Maybe Asha would let me rent a room in her château."

"Wow," Quentin said softly. "Sounds like you've given this a lot of thought, Lex."

"Not before today," she admitted. "But on the drive home from Mom's I had time to reflect, do some soul searching."

"Soul searching," Quentin repeated without inflection. She nodded.

Hazel eyes probed hers. "Was there anything else you… searched your soul about?"

Lexi held his gaze for a long, charged moment. "Not really," she lied.

A shadow crossed his face.

Silence lapsed between them. Stretched uncomfortably.

Quentin was the first to break it. "Well, I should go," he murmured, rising to his feet. "Got some briefs to look over."

"Of course." Lexi swallowed reflexively. "I'll walk you out."

She hopped down from the counter, prepared to follow him out of the room.

Without warning Quentin turned around.

Before she could react, he cupped her face between his big hands and crushed his mouth to hers. She gasped, the heat of his lips sending electric shockwaves through her system. Her hands jerked up to his chest to push him away, but her body overrode the mental command and her arms slid around his neck instead. He growled deep in his throat, the primitive sound igniting her blood.

His arms banded tightly around her waist, drawing her fully against him. His body was hot, hard and powerfully male, reminding her of the contrast in their size and strength.

His tongue licked at her lips, then slid past them to tease the tip of hers. She trembled, parting her lips wider to take him deeper. He plunged inside, his tongue exploring her mouth with hungry, masterful strokes that sent liquid fire racing through her veins, pounding into her sex. She found herself lifting on tiptoe to get even closer to him, to press her aching nipples into his chest, to grind her pelvis against the hard, heavy ridge of his erection.

He dragged his mouth from hers to plant kisses across her cheekbone, muttering raggedly, "I've been trying like hell to forget what you smell like. What you taste like. What you *feel* like." His tongue traced the shell of her ear, making her shiver. "But it's no use. I can't get you out of my mind. I *need* you, Lexi. Need you so damn much."

A whimper of longing escaped her throat.

"You're not leaving me," he growled, his voice rough with anger and desperation. "Not without a damn fight."

Her heart thundered in her chest. "Quentin—"

He took her mouth again, silencing her with a deep, plundering kiss that left her moaning and clinging tightly to him. All these years, she silently marveled. How could she not have known that he was capable of this kind of raw, soul-shattering passion? *How could she not have known?*

He lifted her with breathtaking ease and set her down on the counter, groaning thickly when she wrapped her legs around him. She clung to his big, muscled shoulders as their mouths meshed and parted hungrily, sharing the same warm breath. She was drowning in the taste of him, the intoxicatingly male scent of him. As she ran her hands down his firm, muscled butt, she wondered what it would be like to experience the full power of this desire unleashed, to allow Quentin to make love to her *just once.*

Deepening the kiss, he sank one hand into her short hair, sifting the layered strands through his fingers. With his other hand he reached under her shirt. She shivered as he traced the curves of her body, skimming the underside of her bare breast. He cupped her in his palm, and she cried out at the feel of his fingers kneading her sensitized breast, his thumb brushing across her erect nipple. Need tore through her body.

And finally shocked her back to sanity.

She wrenched her mouth from his, gasping and trembling violently. "No," she whispered. "We can't do this."

He groaned hoarsely. "Lex—"

"*No.* I mean it, Quentin. No more." She flattened her hands against his chest and shoved him away—or at least tried to. He was as immovable as a concrete wall.

Slowly he raised his head to meet her gaze, his bright, heavy-lidded eyes glittering with fierce arousal. Tension radiated from his body. The hard, pounding rhythm of his heart vibrated against her palms.

She dragged in a deep, shaky breath. "You shouldn't have kissed me," she told him with as much composure as she could summon. "And I shouldn't have let you."

"Why not?"

"Why not?" she echoed incredulously. "Because we're friends, Quentin."

"Friends make the best lovers," he murmured, gently stroking a hand down her hair.

Her belly quivered, and she resisted the urge to lean into his touch like a purring, contented cat. Jerking her head away, she said firmly, "Look, what happened in France was a mistake."

"It didn't feel like a mistake," he countered huskily. "And neither did this."

"Well, it was. And it can't happen again. I'm serious, Quentin. Don't push me too hard, or I'll—"

"What?" he taunted, challenge flashing in his eyes. "You'll run away? Pretend this never happened? Good luck with that."

She stared at him, torn between anger and confusion. "Why are you doing this? Why are you trying to ruin our friendship?"

"I'm not," he said softly. "Your friendship means more to me than anything, Lex."

Her heart constricted. "Then don't do this to us, Quentin. *Please.*"

He held her imploring gaze for what seemed an eternity.

Finally he stepped back and helped her down from the counter. But instead of releasing her, he trapped her against the cabinet with his long, muscular legs on either side of hers. Her breath lodged in her throat.

Leaning down, he brushed a tender kiss across her forehead and whispered in her ear, "This isn't over."

She trembled, swallowing hard. "I think it's time for you to go."

But long after he had left, his whispered promise echoed through her mind, taunting and tormenting her.

Because she knew better than anyone how relentless and determined Quentin Reddick could be when he set his sights on having something, whether he was enduring the rigors of pledging a fraternity or earning a law degree. He'd never let anything stop him from pursuing—and getting—what he wanted.

If Lexi were to have any hope of resisting him, her will would have to be stronger than his.

Much stronger.

Otherwise, she was in for a world of heartache.

Chapter 7

"This is Valerie Becker, reporting to you live from the Court of Appeals as we gear up for the fifth day of testimony in one of the biggest whistle-blower trials the state of Georgia has ever seen. The defense's star witness is expected to take the stand today to…"

The woman's excited voice droned on as Lexi hurried past the buzzing crowd of reporters and cameramen gathered on the courthouse steps. She was running late thanks to traffic, which had been even worse than usual that morning.

As she'd stewed in her car, inching along at a maddening crawl, her insides had churned at the thought of seeing Quentin for the first time since they'd shared that explosive kiss at her house nearly a week ago. She'd been so shaken by the kiss that she'd seriously considered not showing up for any part of the trial. But Quentin was her best friend, and this was one of the biggest cases of his career. No matter what had recently transpired between them, she knew how much he'd appreciate having her there to root him on. That's what friends were for.

Once inside the courthouse, Lexi passed through a metal detector and another security checkpoint before making her way quickly to the courtroom. As expected, it was packed, filled with spectators who'd been lured by the prospect of watching a corrupt health-insurance company get its comeuppance.

Standing in the back of the noisy courtroom, Lexi scanned the crowd, hoping against hope that she'd find an empty seat near the front. But after several moments she heaved a sigh of disappointment, knowing she'd have to settle for sitting all the way in the back.

As she moved to claim a spot before even more people arrived, she spied a man rising from his seat near the front, just three rows behind the plaintiff's table. She watched as he strode briskly down the aisle, his expression alarmed as he spoke into the cell phone pressed to his ear.

Seizing the opportunity, Lexi made a beeline to the recently vacated seat before someone else beat her to it. Once settled, she trained her gaze on the plaintiff's table. Her pulse quickened at the sight of Quentin, who was conferring with one of his associates from the law firm, their heads bent close together.

Lexi stared, her eyes tracing the line of Quentin's strong profile to follow the path of his broad shoulders beneath an expensively tailored dark suit. Her belly clenched at the memory of clinging to those shoulders as she and Quentin devoured each other's mouths. She'd wanted him so damn bad. If she hadn't come to her senses and pulled away when she did, there was no telling—

"All rise!" the bailiff called out, interrupting Lexi's

reverie—and not a moment too soon. "The Honorable Judge Clayton Greer, presiding."

Everyone in the courtroom stood as the tall, gray-haired judge emerged from his chambers and took his seat on the bench. His eyes went immediately to Quentin, who was buttoning his suit jacket and smoothing a hand over his silk tie. Meeting the judge's austere gaze, he smiled—a slow, lazy smile that hinted at his irreverent nature.

The judge frowned and shook his head slightly, no doubt wondering for the millionth time what he'd done to land Quentin—a relentless troublemaker—in his courtroom.

Lexi grinned wryly to herself. *I feel your pain, Judge Greer. Believe me, I do.*

Quentin was facing a formidable adversary.

It wasn't the presiding judge, a grizzled relic whose jaundiced glare made it clear he was no fan of Quentin's. And it wasn't the team of smug, high-powered lawyers smirking at him from the table across the aisle.

No, the adversary Quentin faced was fear.

Lexi refused to be with him because she was afraid. She was afraid to jeopardize their friendship. Afraid to trust him. Afraid to get hurt.

So somehow he had to find a way to help her overcome those fears so they could be together. It would definitely be a challenge.

But when had Quentin ever backed down from a challenge?

"Your cross, Mr. Reddick."

Quentin glanced up from the "notes" he'd been furiously scribbling during the defense attorney's direct examination of their star witness. He'd actually been doodling on his yellow legal pad. Depending on the opposition, he often pretended to take copious notes during witness testimonies.

It gave him the appearance of being scattershot, not well prepared. Distracted, even. In reality, he'd heard every word spoken, deciphered every subtle nuance of the witness's voice.

And he knew where he'd launch his attack.

Quentin slowly rose from the table. He never rushed his cue. So he hitched up his pant leg, propped one foot on his chair and proceeded to tie his left shoe.

A wave of chuckles and guffaws spread across the packed courtroom. At the defense table, someone groaned in disbelief.

Quentin hid a wicked grin.

Glancing up from his task, he felt a jolt of surprise when he saw Lexi seated three rows back. After the way they'd parted company last week, he hadn't expected her to show up for any part of the trial. He was deliriously, ridiculously happy to see her.

When their eyes met, she grinned and mouthed, *Go get 'em.*

He winked at her.

"Your Honor," complained the defense team's lead hired gun. "Mr. Reddick is famous for his courtroom shenanigans. Please try to rein him in today."

"With all due respect, Counselor, I'll thank you not to tell me how to run my courtroom. That said—" Judge Greer leveled a stern glare at Quentin "—let's keep the theatrics to a minimum, shall we, Mr. Reddick?"

Quentin blinked, giving him a look of sham innocence. "*Me?* Theatrical?"

A ripple of laughter swept over the courtroom.

The judge jabbed a finger at Quentin. "You've been warned, Counselor."

"Duly noted, Your Honor." He glanced down at the row

of expensive, gleaming Italian loafers marching down the opposition's table.

"Nice shoes," he complimented.

The lead defense attorney gave him a small, patronizing smile. "Whose?"

"All of them."

The audience laughed. A few jurors looked mildly disgusted as they regarded the team of defense attorneys.

Bingo, Quentin thought. Since the trial began, he'd constantly looked for ways to reinforce the perception of the big, bad corporation armed with an arsenal of high-priced goons. The common man versus the greedy insurance giant. David versus Goliath.

Everyone loved an underdog. He was counting on this jury to be no exception.

He sauntered toward the witness stand, where Mary Tanner sat calmly waiting to be cross-examined. Spine erect, shoulders squared, hands folded primly in her lap, she was the picture of perfect composure. She'd been coached, and coached well.

So it was Quentin's job to find the crack in her armor and exploit it to his advantage.

Not unlike what he intended to do with Lexi.

He'd spent years studying the law, just as he'd spent years getting to know Lexi. He knew the inner workings of the legal system, just as he understood the intricacies of Lexi's mind.

So how do you conquer an adversary like fear? By facing it head-on and never backing down. By presenting incontrovertible evidence that the fear is unwarranted. Not unlike the way you'd deal with a child who's afraid of the dark by showing her that there are no monsters hiding under her bed or lurking in the closet. By assuring her that she's safe with you around, that she can rest easy because you'd never let any harm come to her.

And speaking of providing evidence...

"How often have you been promoted in the past year, Ms. Tanner?"

The woman raised a defiant chin. "Twice."

"Twice? Congratulations." Quentin sauntered over to the jury box and casually leaned on the banister. The twelve jurors met his lazy gaze with varying expressions of amusement and admiration. "Just out of curiosity, Ms. Tanner, how often had your predecessor been promoted in the seven years she worked for the company?"

"My predecessor?" she echoed blankly.

"Yes. The woman who occupied your position before you were hired. Would you happen to know how often she was promoted during *her* tenure with the company?"

Silence.

"You don't know?" Quentin prompted.

"Twice," came the low response.

"Twice," he confirmed, deliberately looking each juror in the eye as he meandered down the length of the jury box. "So in the three years you've been with the company, Ms. Tanner, you've already been promoted more times than your predecessor was in seven years. Doesn't that strike you as a bit too...*convenient?*"

"Objection, Your Honor. Counsel is leading the witness. And when did *her* job become the issue here?"

Quentin heaved a bored sigh. "Goes to credibility, Your Honor. The main reason my client lost his job was that Ms. Tanner was trying to preserve her own. In other words, she did her employer's bidding at Mr. Henry's expense."

Judge Greer nodded. "I'll allow it."

"Ms. Tanner?" Quentin prodded, strolling back over to the witness stand.

"I'm good at what I do," she said evenly.

"Yes, you are," Quentin smoothly agreed. "Your department has a *very* high rate of claim denials. You've saved the company quite a lot of money, haven't you?"

"Objection! The company's claim-denial practices are *not* on trial here! We're here to determine whether or not Mr. Henry was wrongfully terminated based on his performance. If Mr. Reddick can't remember that—"

"Sustained, Counselor. Let's not lose focus, Mr. Reddick."

Quentin bowed slightly. "My apologies."

There were a few snickers from the jury box.

"So what *about* Mr. Henry?" Quentin asked, pointing across the room at his client. "*Was* he good at his job, Ms. Tanner?"

She smirked. "Not good enough, obviously."

"Obviously?" Quentin raised his brows at her, then strolled to the plaintiff's table and scooped up a thick folder. Returning to the witness stand, he passed the folder to Mary Tanner, who opened it as reluctantly as if she were opening a cage of vipers. "Do you recognize those documents?"

She nodded.

"Please explain to the court what you're looking at."

She swallowed visibly. "Letters of commendation. Performance-appraisal reports."

"With glowing reviews of Mr. Henry's past job performance. Correct?"

She hesitated. "Yes, that's correct."

"And some of those documents bear your signature. Is that also correct?"

"Yes."

"So, you see," Quentin said silkily, "it's *not* so obvious that Mr. Henry wasn't good at his job, is it, Ms. Tanner?

In fact, isn't it true that your complaints about his work only began when you learned that he'd been speaking out against the company's coverage policies?"

"Objection, Your Honor! Counsel is badgering the witness."

"Overruled. You may proceed, Mr. Reddick."

Quentin smiled narrowly. "Oh, that's all right. I'm good for now, Your Honor."

His point had been made.

He stepped back and began his trademark prowling in front of the witness stand, knowing that every eye was on him, waiting for his next move. He was in control of the courtroom, and he liked that. It kept the opposition off balance.

"Ms. Tanner." He stopped before her. "What is your personal opinion of whistle-blowers?"

She blanched.

"Objection! Counsel is trying to bait the witness into impeaching herself!"

"Well, hell," Quentin drawled in his best Southern good ol' boy impersonation, "I wouldn't be very good at my job if I didn't at least *try*."

Laughter swept across the courtroom. Even the jurors smothered grins.

"Let's move on, Mr. Reddick," the judge dryly instructed.

Quentin grinned. "Moving on."

It was time to go for the kill, and he knew the best way. It was a huge gamble. One that could very well backfire, blow up in his face.

But he'd go for it anyway.

He turned and sauntered back toward his table. His client and Byron Devers, the young associate who'd accompanied Quentin to court, were both staring at him with poker faces. Quentin had groomed them to expect the unexpected.

Lexi was also watching him, riveted. He flashed a quick, lazy smile at her, and she smiled back.

Standing at the table, Quentin made a show of thumbing through a folder, as if he were searching for something specific. "What if I told you, Ms. Tanner, that I'd recently come into possession of an email sent by you to a colleague in another department? In that email, you raved about Mr. Henry's successful handling of a certain project, and you stated that you'd give him a promotion in a heartbeat if it were entirely up to you? What if I told you, Ms. Tanner, that this email was sent *three days* before my client was terminated?"

He was bluffing, of course. The "colleague" he'd referenced had been too afraid of retaliation to testify against her employer. So he didn't have any actual email exchanges to furnish as evidence.

But it didn't matter.

In the second before the lead defense attorney jumped to his feet to object to the introduction of new evidence, Mary Tanner burst out defensively, "You don't understand how much pressure we're under to—" She caught herself.

But it was too late.

A hushed silence fell over the courtroom.

Quentin brought his head up slowly, his brows arched inquiringly. "How much pressure you're under to do *what*, Ms. Tanner?" he prompted softly.

She clamped her lips together and darted an apologetic glance toward the defense table.

Noise erupted in the courtroom as the gathered spectators and reporters reacted to her damning near-admission. Judge Greer banged his gavel, calling for order.

"Your Honor," the lead defense attorney implored, "in light of this development, we'd like to request a short recess to, ah, regroup."

"I figured you would, Counselor" was the judge's droll response.

Quentin's client was grinning from ear to ear. And Lexi was giving him a thumbs-up sign, her face glowing with pride.

Quentin smiled at her.

Watch out, Lexi. I'm coming for you next.

Chapter 8

That evening, Quentin invited Lexi and their friends out for dinner and drinks to celebrate how well the trial was going. A court case of this magnitude ordinarily took at least four weeks. In light of the day's surprise development, everyone believed that a favorable verdict for Quentin's whistle-blower client was a foregone conclusion.

Lexi and Quentin were the first to arrive at the upscale downtown restaurant. After the gushing hostess requested Quentin's autograph, he and Lexi were escorted to a posh VIP lounge and served cocktails while they waited for the rest of their party to join them.

Although it had been hard to keep her distance from Quentin for the past six days, Lexi was glad she'd toughed it out. He'd needed to concentrate on the trial, and *she'd* needed time to recover from their last explosive encounter and shore up her defenses. Now, seated beside him on the plush sofa—not within kissing distance—she felt reasonably in control of herself and the situation. Of course, knowing that they wouldn't be alone much longer certainly helped.

Reflecting on the drama that had unfolded that day in the courtroom, she smiled and shook her head. "No matter how many times I've seen you in action, Quentin, you never cease to amaze me."

He chuckled softly, lounging on the sofa with one arm draped across the back of the seat cushion and a glass of whiskey cradled in the other hand, which bore his gold class ring from Morehouse. He still wore his impeccably tailored Gucci suit, but he'd removed his tie and loosened the top three buttons of his shirt, exposing the strong, masculine column of his throat. He looked utterly relaxed and content, a man at his leisure.

He also looked drop-dead sexy.

Shoving the unwelcome thought from her mind, Lexi continued, "Seriously. I've already told you a thousand times what a gifted, brilliant trial lawyer you are. You're absolutely riveting. But I swear, Quentin, you say and do some of the most outrageous things sometimes. I mean, only *you* would stop to tie your shoes, then compliment the other guys' shoes, before cross-examining a hostile witness."

Quentin grinned, tapping a broad finger to his temple. "It's psychological."

"I know. Everything you do in that courtroom is calculated." She'd seen him manipulate and seduce women with the same finesse. It was downright frightening.

"But all kidding aside," he said soberly. "I really want to win this case. My client stood up for what he believed in, and it cost him his job and his good reputation. These health insurance companies are controlling people's lives— deciding whether they live or die—based on how much profit they stand to gain. It makes me sick to my damn stomach. If I can't get these greedy bastards convicted for their corrupt policies, then taking a pound of their flesh is the next best thing."

Lexi gazed at him, goose bumps peppering her skin. One of the things she'd always admired about Quentin was his fiery intensity. He was passionate about his beliefs, his innate sense of right and wrong. He'd gone into law to become an advocate for those who couldn't advocate for themselves. Lexi used to tease him back in college, telling him that beneath his devil-may-care playboy persona beat the heart of a righteous crusader.

Smiling softly at him, she said, "Your client is very lucky to have you on his side."

Quentin met her gaze. "And *I'm* lucky to have you on mine. Thanks for coming today, Lex. I really appreciated seeing you there."

The tender gratitude on his face made her heart squeeze tightly. Averting her eyes, she took a sip of her apple martini and said gruffly, "Don't get all sentimental on me, Red. It's not like I haven't been coming to your trials for years."

"I know," he said quietly. "You've been there from the very beginning, and I want you to know how much that means to me."

She drank more of her martini, swallowing hard.

"Remember my first court case?" Quentin reminisced with a soft chuckle. "I was fresh out of law school, and so damn nervous that I kept mispronouncing the judge's name and repeating the same questions during cross-examination."

Lexi smiled. "You were adorable."

He grimaced. "I was a wreck."

"That, too." She laughed. "But you certainly weren't too nervous to flirt with the court reporter."

"Did I?" His mouth twitched. "I don't remember."

"I do. And I can only imagine what her transcript looked like by the time you were through with her. You might have gotten that poor woman fired, Quentin."

"I hope not."

"Me too." Lexi grinned, then sighed. "Well, you've definitely come a long way as a litigator."

He gazed at her. "A lot has changed over the years."

She blushed, fully aware that he was referring to their relationship. Taking a sip of her drink, she murmured, "Not everything has to change."

"Change can be good." His voice deepened. "Very good."

She'd somehow misjudged the reach of his long arm draped over the sofa. Before she realized it, his thumb was rubbing the nape of her neck with small, lazy circles that sent shivers down her spine. As her nipples tightened and bolts of sensation zigzagged to her groin, she wondered how such a simple caress could wreak pure havoc on her body. Why couldn't all these pulsing nerves have remained dormant, forever immune to his touch?

She checked her watch, then cast a desperate glance at the empty doorway. "I can't believe everyone's running so late. It's not like them, especially Reese. She's Ms. Punctuality."

Quentin took a languid sip of his whiskey. "They're not coming."

She looked at him in surprise. "They're not?"

"No."

"How do you know?" She fumbled out her cell phone. "I don't have any missed calls. Did one of them call or text you?"

"No." He met her puzzled gaze. "They're not coming, because I never invited them."

"You didn't inv—?" As comprehension dawned, she stared at him in disbelief. "You set this whole thing up just so I'd have dinner with you?"

"Pretty much."

She scowled. "I don't believe you! Resorting to trickery to get your way? That's *so* underhanded."

Quentin gave her a knowing look. "If I'd asked you out to dinner—just the two of us—would you have accepted?"

She hesitated. "No."

"I rest my case."

They stared each other down.

"I have to use the bathroom," she blurted, lunging to her feet.

As she strode quickly from the room, Quentin called out, "Lexi."

She stopped and glanced back at him.

He was studying the twinkling contents of his glass. "Don't run out on me."

Hearing the veiled warning in his voice, she swallowed. "I won't."

But the thought crossed her mind as she lingered in the restroom—retouching her lipstick, combing her hair, doing everything possible to delay her return to him. Why *shouldn't* she leave the restaurant? Quentin knew she was adamantly opposed to elevating their relationship, yet he'd tricked her into having dinner with him anyway. It would serve him right if she left him high and dry. And she could, since they'd arrived in separate cars.

So what was stopping her?

"Good manners," Lexi muttered to her reflection. "Loyalty. A guilty conscience. A big appetite."

She sighed. *None of the above.*

Against her better judgment, she wanted to spend the

evening with Quentin. After six days apart, she missed him. Missed him more than she should have.

"God help me," she whispered.

Knowing she couldn't hide in the restroom all night, she mentally squared her shoulders and headed out the door.

The solicitous maître d' was waiting to escort her back to Quentin. But instead of being led to a table in the main dining area, Lexi was taken to one of the restaurant's private rooms. As soon as she stepped through the door, she gasped sharply.

The room's elegant decor featured marble columns and gleaming parquet floors. The walls were hung with mirrors and lush artwork that captured the French countryside. Lights from a crystal chandelier were dimmed intimately low, while candles glowed on the linen-covered table. Nearby, a pair of double doors led onto a terrace that overlooked the glittering night skyline. The soft strains of classic French music could be heard in the background.

"Ohhh," Lexi breathed, gazing around in utter amazement. She'd been transported back to France.

Quentin rose from behind a baby grand piano tucked into the corner, where he'd been plucking out a few errant chords. He couldn't play a lick, but vowed to learn someday.

"There you are." He came toward her slowly, his gaze latched onto hers. "I was starting to think you'd bolted on me."

"I considered it." But her voice broke, and to her dismay, tears welled in her eyes. "Quentin. This is... I can't believe..." She shook her head, too choked up to continue.

"Don't cry," he murmured, humor threading his deep voice. "At least not until you've tasted the food."

She let out a teary laugh. Her heart was so full it felt as though it'd burst out of her chest at any moment.

Quentin took her hand and led her over to the table by the French doors. He pulled out her chair, and when she sat down, he gently pushed it back in, making her feel as cherished and delicate as fine china.

As he claimed his own seat, she braced her elbows on the table, rested her forehead on her clasped hands and drew a deep, shaky breath, praying for composure. When she raised her head again, she found Quentin watching her with an expression of tender adoration.

Before she could speak, a waiter appeared with a bottle of Chablis and a platter of French cheeses. To Lexi's delight, the young man spoke flawless French. After pouring their wine and conversing with them for a few minutes, he departed with the promise to return shortly with their meals.

When Lexi and Quentin were alone again, she asked incredulously, "*When* did you plan all this? You've been tied up with the trial since we got back from our trip!"

He gave her an amused look. "I know how to multitask."

"Obviously." She swept an awed glance around the room. "This is absolutely amazing, Quentin. The paintings, the terrace, the music. Even the French-speaking waiter. I feel like we're back in Burgundy."

"Good," he said softly. "That was the point. Since we didn't get a chance to visit one of those world-renowned restaurants while we were in France, I figured I'd make it up to you."

Her heart expanded even more. "But it wasn't your fault. *I'm* the one who harangued Asha into letting me and Michael cook dinner for everyone on our last night there."

"I know." Quentin smiled wryly. "And I was really looking forward to that meal you promised me when we got home."

She gave him an abashed grin. "Rain check?"

"Definitely." Eyes glinting with mirth, he gently swirled his glass and nosed the wine as she'd taught him.

"No choking," she warned, and they both laughed.

A thought occurred to her. "Wait a minute. How are we having French food? This isn't even a French restaurant."

Quentin smiled lazily. "I know. But they had this great room with a view, and they were able to accommodate my needs on short notice. As for what we're eating tonight, it pays to have more than one friend who's a chef. Mike pulled some strings for me, so I think you'll be very pleased with what we're served."

Enthralled, Lexi shook her head at him. "You know you're not playing fair, right?"

"I never said I would." He raised his glass to her. "To Burgundy."

She smiled softly. "And unforgettable memories."

They clinked glasses and sipped, gazing at each other. Soft candlelight flickered across Quentin's strong, handsome face and illuminated his hazel eyes. She'd always taken for granted how remarkable his eyes were, how arrestingly beautiful and mesmerizing. Now she found herself drowning in them.

"What're you thinking about?" Quentin murmured.

"Your eyes," she admitted. "They're incredible."

"So are yours. I can't stop thinking about them." His voice dipped low. "Or the rest of you, for that matter."

Her belly quivered. She drank more wine.

"Your eyes are the first thing I noticed about you when we met," Quentin told her.

She was surprised. "Really?"

He nodded, idly tracing the rim of his glass with one finger. "It was freshman year, and we were at that off-campus party. It was crowded—"

"So you found a cozy corner to make out with some girl," Lexi interjected with a wry smile.

"Don't interrupt."

"Sorry."

"Anyway," Quentin continued pointedly. "Yes, I was in a corner getting better acquainted with a young lady—"

Lexi snorted at that. "'Better acquainted.'"

Quentin scowled. "Are you gonna let me finish?"

"Sorry." She bit her lip to stifle a grin. "By all means. Please continue."

"Thank you." Humor tugged at the corners of his mouth. "As I was saying, the young lady and I were getting better acquainted. But as I leaned in to make my move, something else caught my eye. I glanced up, and there was this pretty little tenderoni moving slowly through the crowd. She was searching for someone, and I took one look into her eyes and hoped it was me."

Lexi stared at him, her insides tingling with pleasure. They'd reminisced about their first meeting many times over the years, but this was the first time she'd ever heard *this* version.

"She had the most beautiful, exotic eyes I'd ever seen," Quentin continued softly. "I won't lie. They took my breath away. And when the rest of her face came into view, it only got better. Our eyes met, and she gave me this sweet, shy smile—"

"*Before* she saw the girl in your arms, who definitely was *not* smiling when she realized you had a wandering eye."

Quentin grinned sheepishly. "Well, anyway, to make a long story short, the tenderoni's smile quickly turned into a frown, and with a disgusted roll of those stunning eyes, she moved on without a backward glance. Later, when we were introduced to each other by Mike—who'd apparently made a better first impression than I had—the tenderoni laughed at one of my jokes. And that's how I eventually won her over."

Lexi chuckled, nibbling on a piece of Chaource cheese. "Yep. That sounds about right." She hesitated, then couldn't resist adding, "I didn't know that was your first impression of me. You never hit on me after that night."

Quentin looked amused. "Is that a question or a complaint?"

She blushed. "Neither. I'm just making an observation."

He chuckled, low and soft. "For starters, you made it perfectly clear what you thought of my, ah, wandering eye. I figured I'd only be setting myself up for rejection if I tried to make a move on you. And once we got to know each other better, I realized that having your friendship was more important to me than trying to get you into bed."

Lexi gazed at him, her heart constricting. "I think that's the sweetest thing you've ever said to me, Quentin."

"Naw," he guffawed, leaning back in his chair. "I'm pretty sure I've said *much* sweeter things than that."

She laughed, even as his previous words echoed through her mind. *She was searching for someone, and I took one look into her eyes and hoped it was me.*

She shivered convulsively. The man definitely had a way with words.

Reaching for another piece of cheese, she gave him a small, whimsical smile. "Just out of curiosity, what was the second thing you noticed about me?"

Quentin's eyes glinted wickedly. "Your ass."

Sputtering with indignation, Lexi threw her cheese at him.

They were still laughing and teasing each other when the waiter returned with their meals. He set the plates on the table with a flourish and identified each dish: wine-poached salmon with black truffles, cognac shrimp with beurre blanc sauce and foie gras with figs. Lexi was delighted with the classic French food, which she and Quentin proceeded to share, sometimes eating from the same plate at the same time.

They talked throughout dinner. Even after all these years, Lexi marveled that they never ran out of things to say to each other. There was a natural flow to their conversation, the relaxed camaraderie shared by two people who could complete each other's sentences, even when they chose not to. At the same time, Lexi couldn't help wondering how it was possible to feel so comfortable with a man who set her blood on fire.

They'd just finished dessert—an exquisite parfait glacé aux marrons—when a romantic Viennese waltz began playing in the background. Suddenly Lexi was transported back to the night of the masquerade ball.

Quentin rose from his chair and rounded the table to stand over her, his hand outstretched to her. "I believe you still owe me a dance."

Her heart thudded at the deep, intoxicating timbre of his voice. In the far recesses of her mind, she knew she should just thank him for the wonderful dinner and call it a night while she still could.

Instead she smiled, placed her hand in his and murmured, "I believe you're right."

Quentin led her out to the middle of the floor and drew her into his arms. She melted at once, curving her arms around his neck and settling her head against the broad wall of his chest. The dramatic difference in their heights should have made their dancing awkward. But they swayed together as easily and gracefully as if their movements had been specially choreographed by the great George Balanchine.

Years of practice, Lexi rationalized. They'd danced together a thousand times over the course of their friendship. But tonight was different. She felt it as surely as Quentin did.

"When was the last time we did this?" he murmured, his cheek resting against the top of her head.

"Danced together?"

"Yeah."

"Michael's wedding."

"Then it's been too damn long."

A secret thrill of pleasure curled through Lexi, and she smiled.

His strong, muscled thighs rubbed against hers as he turned her slowly in a circle, keeping one hand at the small of her back and the other firmly around her waist. She could feel his steady heartbeat, the lift of his chest with every breath he took. She relished the warmth of his body surrounding her.

She didn't want the romantic waltz to end. She didn't want the night to end. She was completely caught up in the profound perfection of the moment.

So she didn't mind when the hand at her waist urged her closer. She simply closed her eyes and let out a soft sigh. A moment later Quentin ran his other hand up her back, a whisper of sensation against the silk of her blouse. Her breasts tingled, her nipples puckering against his hard chest.

She felt his breathing change at the same time hers quickened.

She lifted her head and stared up at him. Though the lights were dimmed low, there was no mistaking the flare of hunger in the glittering eyes that stared back at her. Her heart thumped against her breastbone.

Cradling her face between his hands, Quentin brushed his lips across her forehead, her closed eyelids, her nose and her cheekbones before claiming her mouth. Lexi trembled, her senses reeling from the fiercely tender assault. She kissed him back, hungrily seeking the heat and flavor of his mouth.

As their tongues tangled sensually, he stroked a hand down her body and cupped her bottom. She moaned. Her blood poured through her veins like heated wine, leaving her feeling flushed and slightly intoxicated.

As Quentin gently kneaded her butt, she leaned up on tiptoe until her aching groin cradled the hard, thick bulge of his erection. He groaned, holding her tightly against him while his mouth devoured hers with searing intensity. Her heart thundered, squeezing the air out of her lungs.

"Lex," he whispered raggedly. "I *want* you. Tell me what I have to do to have you."

The words jarred her back to reality.

She tore her mouth from his and stared up at him. The raw hunger on his face mirrored the desire rampaging through her body. She wanted him, wanted him so badly she shook with it. It would have been so easy to surrender to temptation, to go home with him and let him make love to her. She ached to feel his body joined with hers, possessing her.

But it was too dangerous.

"I—I can't," she stammered, shaking her head.

"Lex—"

Quentin took a step toward her and she retreated

backward. "I'm sorry. This was such an incredible evening. Everything was perfect. But I can't do this, Quentin."

He stared down at her, his eyes smoldering with sexual need and frustration.

"I should go." It was more plea than declaration.

He held her gaze for another long, electrified moment, then heaved a resigned breath and muttered, "At least let me walk you to your damn car."

She knew better than to argue.

Chapter 9

But she argued with herself on the drive home. Or rather, she argued with her raging libido, which tormented her with throbbing breasts and a deep, relentless ache between her thighs that had her squirming and wanting to climb out of her skin.

She was halfway home before she finally accepted defeat.

"Screw this." With barely a glance in her rearview mirror, she hooked a hard U-turn at the next traffic light and headed back toward midtown. By the time she reached the luxury high-rise on Peachtree Street, she was breathless with anticipation, adrenaline and lust.

She swung into the underground parking garage, inserted a coded key card to open the gate, then wheeled her car into the empty guest spot that practically belonged to her. Spying Quentin's black Jaguar, she nodded with satisfaction.

Inside the lobby, her stiletto heels clicked smartly on the polished marble floor as she strode to the bank of elevators, the flaps of her belted trench coat blowing open across her legs.

"Good evening, Miss Austin," the concierge said as she sailed past him with a distracted smile and a wave.

The elevator whisked her up to the twentieth floor in seconds, but even that wasn't fast enough. When she reached Quentin's penthouse at the end of the corridor, she pressed the doorbell and waited, shaking with nerves and excitement. When there was no response, she quickly punched numbers into the combination keypad. As soon as the lock clicked open, she stepped inside and closed the door behind her.

Then, and only then, did she have a moment's pause.

Could she really go through with this?

Too late for second thoughts now. You're already in the lion's den.

Breathing deeply to bolster her flagging courage, Lexi set her purse on the foyer table and swept a cursory glance around the two-story penthouse, which boasted gleaming mahogany floors, ultramodern fixtures and masculine, contemporary furnishings. A wall of windows commanded a stunning view of downtown Atlanta, now blanketed with glittering lights.

"Lexi?"

Her gaze swung across the shadowy living room, where Quentin was slowly descending a spiral staircase. Her pulse hammered at the base of her throat.

He reached the landing and stepped into a soft pool of light. He'd changed for bed, putting on a pair of long black shorts and nothing else. Her mouth ran dry at the sight of his massive shoulders and wide chest sculpted with hard, sinewy muscle. It wasn't the first time she'd seen him shirtless, but tonight she intended to explore every inch of all that glorious male flesh.

"I thought I heard the doorbell." He stared at her, his eyes shadowed and heavy lidded. "What're you doing here, Lex?"

She met his gaze directly. "I changed my mind."

Silence.

"You changed your mind." His voice was a deep, husky rumble in the semidarkness.

She gulped. "Yes."

Another pause. Then came his faintly amused drawl, "Is that why you're still hiding by the front door?"

An embarrassed flush heated her face. So much for all her bravado.

Quentin started toward her. "So what changed your mind, Alexis?"

He only called her by her full name when he was angry or deadly serious about something.

She licked her dry lips. "I don't know."

"You don't know." His slow, stealthy advance reminded her of a hunter who's sighted his prey and wants to make certain it doesn't escape. "Are you sure you don't know?"

Swallowing, she unglued her feet from the floor and took a brave step forward. "I want you," she whispered.

He stopped moving. "I didn't hear you. Speak up."

So that's how he wants to play this. Okay. You probably had it coming.

"I want you," she said in a clearer, stronger voice. "I've thought of nothing but you since the night of that damn New Year's Eve ball. I came here tonight against my better judgment because I can't seem to help myself. I want to make love with my best friend. But if you're going to play games—"

As she reached for the door, he lunged.

Her breath whooshed out of her lungs as he hauled her roughly into his arms and crushed his mouth to hers. The kiss was raw and blistering, the heat of his big, hard body scorching her from the inside out. She flung her arms around his neck and opened her mouth, sucking his hot, thrusting tongue with a hunger that staggered them both.

He pushed her back against the door and quickly hoisted her off the floor. She threw her legs around his waist, hiking her skirt up to her thighs as her stilettos clattered to the floor. He grabbed her butt, roughly palming both cheeks as he ground his rigid erection against her sex. She moaned, writhing against him as fingers of electrical explosions tore through her clitoris.

He reared back and impatiently ripped off her trench coat. Her nipples stood out sharply against her pale silk blouse. Nostrils flaring, he bent his head and sucked one into his hot, wet mouth. She arched back, keening with pleasure.

He kneaded and caressed her thighs, the rough heat of his skin penetrating her pantyhose. But it wasn't enough; she wanted his hands on her bare flesh. As if he'd read her mind, he eased her feet to the floor, then sank to his knees before her. His fingers gripped the waistband of her pantyhose, yanking it past the swell of her hips and rolling it down her legs. She trembled uncontrollably, her breath rushing in and out of her lungs. When he reached her feet, she stepped out of the hose, then watched as he brought the nylon to his nose and deeply inhaled.

"It smells like you," he whispered thickly.

She groaned, shuddering with arousal.

Setting aside the wad of pantyhose, he leaned forward and brushed his lips to the sensitive flesh of her inner thigh. She moaned, delicious shivers racing to her groin. Holding her skirt out of the way, he trailed a path of sensual, open-mouthed kisses up her trembling thigh. When he reached her crotch he paused, heightening her anticipation. And then he pressed his tongue to her clit, stroking her through the silk layer of her panties. She cried out hoarsely.

As her knees buckled he caught her, steadying her in his firm grasp.

"Quentin," she whimpered, writhing desperately against him as wetness coated her sex. "I *need* you."

He lifted his head and stared up at her. His face was flushed, his eyes bright and gleaming with barely restrained lust.

"Not here," he growled huskily. "Not for our first time."

He surged to his feet, then bent and swept her into his arms as though she were completely weightless. She clung to his neck and pressed her hot face against his chest, feeling small and vulnerable and powerfully outmatched.

He reached the second landing in what had to be record time and carried her into his enormous bedroom, where a lamp glowed invitingly on the bedside table.

He set her gently on the floor and slanted his mouth over hers, his kiss as hot and hungry as the sensual needs pounding through her body. His hands caressed her back, stroking the silk of her blouse against her tingling flesh. Without breaking the kiss, he unbuttoned her shirt with a deftness that reminded her he'd had plenty of practice undressing women. But at that moment she didn't give a damn. She wanted to be naked and joined with him, and the sooner the better.

Lifting his head, he dragged her blouse off her shoulders, then reached for the front clasp of her bra. Her breath caught at the sensation of silk brushing against her erect nipples. Pulse thundering, she watched Quentin's face as he eased the straps down her arms and pushed the bra from her body. At the sight of her brazenly thrusting nipples, his nostrils flared and he swallowed tightly.

She gasped as his hands cupped her swollen breasts, his thumbs rasping over her distended nipples. Her womb contracted as spasms of pleasure tore through her. She'd never known her breasts could be so sensitive. They never had been before.

Swearing under his breath, Quentin knelt to unzip her skirt and slide it, along with her panties, down her legs. She could tell that he was trying to take his time with her, trying to savor her the way a connoisseur savored a fine wine.

When she stood naked and trembling before him, his gaze raked over her slowly, his eyes smoldering with fierce appreciation.

"So this is what I've been missing all these years," he murmured, low and rough. "Have mercy."

Lexi's knees went weak.

As he lifted her, she wrapped her arms around his neck, shivering at the feel of his bare chest pressed against hers. A moment later she felt him lowering her to the enormous bed and easing over her, his heavy body enveloping her with his heat and strength.

She trembled everywhere he touched her, with his hands and his eyes. He palmed her aching breasts, pushing them together. And then he lowered his head and sucked her nipple into his mouth. She gasped and arched backward.

As his marauding lips closed in on the other nipple, his hand glided down to the apex of her thighs. She moaned as his fingers teased and probed the slick, swollen folds of her sex. She thrust her hips against him, shaking with need. And when he slipped two fingers inside her, she cried out and clamped her thighs around his hand, trapping him there.

"So juicy," he groaned low, his lips caressing her jaw as he stroked inside her. "So damn sweet and *juicy*."

She mewled with pleasure, her hips undulating against him as she rode his wicked fingers.

"I need to taste you." He glided down her body, his lips moving between her breasts and down her quivering belly as she struggled for breath. He settled between her thighs, his massive shoulders spreading them wide.

"So beautiful," he whispered hoarsely, his lips poised over her clitoris. "All these years. *All these years.*"

He lifted those glittering eyes, his gaze locking with hers. And then he pressed his hot mouth to her engorged sex. Her hips arched off the bed as a strangled cry erupted from her throat. His hand gripped her waist, anchoring her in place, giving her no reprieve from the sensual onslaught to come.

He suckled her clit as his fingers worked inside her, thrusting with deep, erotic strokes. Lexi twisted, dug her heels into the bed and clutched the back of his head, the silky texture of his close-cut hair rasping her palms. Soon she was groaning and shaking, shuddering from the gut-wrenching pleasure of his mouth on her. Just when she thought she couldn't possibly take any more without dying, he did something with his tongue, something that should be illegal in all U.S. states and territories.

Her eyes flew wide-open, and she screamed his name as waves of violent ecstasy crashed through her, racking her body with such powerful convulsions she seriously wondered whether she'd go into cardiac arrest.

Quentin gathered her against him, his expression both tender and savagely aroused as he watched her come for what seemed an eternity.

When the tremors had finally tapered off, she stared up at him with a look of astonished wonder. She'd always known he was an experienced lover, but she couldn't have imagined the depths to which he'd master her body, making it weep.

As she watched, he slid his fingers from her vagina and slowly drew them into his mouth. The blatant carnality of the gesture sent ripples of lust charging through her belly.

"Sweetness," he husked, holding her gaze as he sucked his wet fingers. *"Sweetness."*

Lexi blushed with pleasure, his pet name for her taking on a whole new meaning.

Bending his head, he captured her mouth in a deep, provocative kiss that had her moaning as she tasted herself on his lips and tongue.

Drawing back from her, he rose to his knees and pulled down his shorts. She gasped, her eyes widening as she got her very first look at his penis. It was an absolute thing of beauty. Long, thick and honest-to-goodness *huge,* curving up toward his stomach.

No wonder women keep coming back for more, Lexi thought as her mouth watered and her clit tightened and throbbed with greedy anticipation.

He retrieved a foil packet from the bedside table, tore it open with his teeth and quickly rolled the condom over that bulging erection. She quivered as he stroked his fingers between her legs, then smeared her juices over the condom. As he slipped between her thighs, a shudder rippled through her as the engorged head of his penis nudged the slippery folds of her sex. She wrapped her legs around his waist, wanting him inside her.

Poised above her, his weight braced on both arms and his hands on either side of her head, Quentin gazed down at her. The piercing, focused intensity in his eyes let her know that he recognized the profound significance of this moment. Just one thrust of his hips would take them from friends to lovers. And there would be no turning back.

But Lexi knew that they'd long since passed the point of no return.

So she gave a slight nod, and something like relief and gratitude flashed across Quentin's face.

They stared into each other's eyes as he slowly pushed inside her, stretching her almost unbearably. They shuddered and groaned in mutual ecstasy. Slowly he sank deeper, sheathing himself to the base. The pleasure was so sharp, so excruciatingly intense, that they shared a heated look and whispered at the same time, "Don't come yet."

They both laughed, soft, shaky laughs that quickly turned into groans as Quentin began moving inside her. She tightened her thighs around him and wrapped her arms around his back, so broad her fingers couldn't meet in a circle. He groaned again as she caught his rhythm, her hips surging upward to meet each deep, penetrating stroke.

"Ah, Lex. Lex, *Lex,*" he chanted, his low, raspy voice driving her insane. "You feel so damn incredible."

"So do you," she moaned.

"Is it good, sweetness?"

"*Sooo* good."

As he groaned and thrust deeper, her nails raked his back and dug into the flexing muscles of his taut, round butt. His erection was so hard it felt like hot iron wedged inside her. Passion and hunger blazed in his eyes, matching the currents of electricity tearing through her. No man had ever made Lexi feel this way before. And she knew, instinctively, that no other man ever would.

Soon she was sobbing Quentin's name and arching her back, her hips working frantically against his as he plunged and retreated. His lips lowered to her breasts, sucking her engorged nipples until she wailed with pleasure. They glided and rocked together, their primal cries and shouts bounding up to the high ceiling and reverberating around the large room.

Framing her face between his hands, Quentin stared down at Lexi with an expression of such fierce possession that tears swam into her eyes. "You mean everything to me," he growled huskily. "Don't you *ever* forget that."

"I won't," she promised, her voice breaking with emotion. There was nothing about this night she could, or would, ever forget.

As his thrusts came harder and faster, Quentin took her mouth in a searing, ravenous kiss that shook her down to her very soul. Pressure built in her womb, a storm gathering force.

Lifting his head, he gazed deep into her eyes and whispered, "Fly with me, Lexi."

And she did, the two of them shattering together and soaring higher than any hot-air balloon could ever take them.

Later, after another round of intense lovemaking, they lay spent in each other's arms, sweat cooling on their bodies, their legs twined beneath the covers that Quentin had pulled up to their waists.

In quiet wonder Lexi explored him, running her hands over the hard-honed muscle that ridged his chest and abdomen. His golden skin was rich and beautiful, as warm and smooth as granite wrapped in silk. A faint smile touched her lips as she traced the ink outline of the Omega Psi Phi tattoo that curved around his bicep. She remembered how proud he'd been the day he received it, remembered the way she'd teased him as she helped him clean and care for the fresh wound.

Looking up into his face, she found him watching her intently beneath the long, thick fringe of his lashes. "So much history between us," she whispered.

His gaze softened. "I know. It's amazing."

"It is." She sighed contentedly. "Do you really think friends make the best lovers?"

A lazy smile touched his lips. "I think we just proved that, don't you?"

She blushed, burying her hot face against his chest.

He laughed, a deep, husky rumble that vibrated through her body. "Don't get all shy on me now."

"I'm not." She muffled a smile against him. She loved the way his skin smelled—a hint of spice from his cologne, mingled with a musky layer of sweat from their fevered lovemaking. She wished that she could bottle the intoxicating scent. She wished she could preserve everything about this incredible night.

Quentin tightened his arm around her, snuggling her closer to his warm body. As she tucked her head beneath his chin, he played with her hair, running his fingers through the short, layered strands.

"I really like your hair this way," he murmured.

She grinned. "It grew on you, huh?"

"What do you mean? I've always liked it."

"Really? I didn't think you were too crazy about it at first. You kept staring at me funny."

"That's because I was in shock. It was a dramatic change. Your hair went from here—" he drew a line just below her shoulders "—to here." He touched the nape of her neck. "It caught me by surprise. But I really like the haircut, Lex. It's sexy as hell, and it brings out those stunning eyes of yours."

Warm pleasure tingled through her veins. She smiled against his chest. "I'm glad you feel that way. It would've been nice to hear this, say, a year ago, but better late than never."

He kissed the top of her head. "I'm sorry. I thought I told you."

"Nope." Apparently there was a lot he hadn't told her, she mused, remembering the story he'd shared about the first time they met. *She was searching for someone, and I took one look into her eyes and hoped it was me.*

For as long as she lived, she would never forget those words.

"I've been meaning to ask you something," Quentin murmured, lazily stroking a hand up and down her spine.

"What?"

"When I kissed you at the New Year's Eve ball, you didn't know it was me. So who *did* you think was kissing you?"

Her face heated at the memory. "I don't know," she mumbled.

"What do you mean?"

"I don't know who I thought was kissing me."

"Are you sure? Maybe you thought it was some guy you'd been flirting with all night."

Hearing the jealous edge to his voice, Lexi laughed. "That's right. We'd planned to meet for a secret rendezvous at the stroke of midnight. But *you* came along and ruined everything."

Quentin's hand stilled on her back. "That's not funny, Lex."

"Oh, relax. I'm just teasing you." She sighed deeply. "The truth is, I'd been feeling a bit sorry for myself that evening. No matter how fabulous a New Year's Eve party is, it's easy to get lonely if you don't have a date. That's why I was out on the terrace." She hesitated, then added shyly, "When you took me into your arms and kissed me, it just seemed so romantic and exciting. What girl doesn't fantasize about being swept off her feet by a mysterious, dashing stranger?"

Quentin said quietly, "And then you realized it wasn't a stranger after all."

"Mmm." She lifted her head and met his steady gaze. "For the record, that was the most amazing New Year's Eve kiss I've ever received."

He smiled softly, brushing his thumb across her lower lip. "I'll never forget it. Or this night."

Neither will I, Lexi thought as their mouths met in an achingly tender kiss. *Neither will I.*

Chapter 10

The next morning, Lexi was awakened by the warmth of Quentin's lips gently nibbling her earlobe. She sighed, a slow, delicious languor spreading through her limbs.

"Good morning." His low, sleep-roughened voice rumbled against her ear, curling her toes and sending tingles to her stomach.

"Good morning." Without opening her eyes she stretched, rubbing her backside along his warm, muscular body spooning hers.

Quentin groaned, his penis hardening against her bottom. "See what you started, woman? And I was gonna let you sleep in this morning."

"How? By assaulting my earlobe?"

He chuckled softly, nuzzling her neck. His warm breath made her shiver. "Take a shower with me."

She groaned protestingly. "But I want to sleep in. You promised I could."

"I changed my mind."

"Too bad," she retorted with a smile. "It's Tuesday. I don't have class until this afternoon. It's not *my* fault you have to be at the office at the crack of dawn, Counselor."

"Don't make me seduce you," he warned silkily, brushing the head of his erection across her butt. As heat bloomed between her thighs, she laughed and scooted out of reach.

Growling softly, Quentin hooked his arm over her waist and turned her around to face him. Dark stubble covered his jaw, making him look so rakishly sexy her breath caught.

He leaned down and kissed her, a sweet, soft kiss that opened up something deep inside her. Something she was afraid to identify.

Lifting his head, he smiled into her eyes. "Hey, sweetness."

She smiled shyly. "Hey."

"Sleep good?"

"When? You kept me up practically all night."

He grinned wolfishly. "I didn't hear you complaining last night."

And he never would, she thought. The man knew how to handle his business, and then some.

"So, listen, I was thinking we could stay in tonight," he suggested, idly running his fingers through her tousled bangs. "Maybe order some takeout and rent a movie."

Striving to match his casual tone, Lexi said, "Sure. That sounds like a plan."

"Good." His eyes glinted. "And I want a rain check on that shower, woman."

"So bossy," she grumbled.

"Damn straight." He gave her a quick, hard kiss, then rolled away and swung his long legs over the edge of the bed. As he sauntered lazily to the master bathroom, Lexi propped her head in her hand and shamelessly admired the view of his naked backside—wide shoulders, round butt, powerful thighs and toned calves.

Um-mmm-umph!

As he disappeared into the bathroom, she let out a lusty sigh and fell back against her pillows with a lascivious grin.

Moments later she heard the blast of the shower. When Quentin began crooning an off-key version of "A Whole New World," she stared at the door in delighted surprise, then dissolved into laughter.

As she snuggled back under the warm covers and tried to grab a few more winks of sleep, Quentin's cell phone buzzed on the bedside table, signaling that he had an incoming text message.

Lexi ignored it and closed her eyes.

Half a minute later, she heard another buzz. She opened her eyes and leveled a glare at the phone. It wasn't his BlackBerry, which he reserved for business. This was his personal cell phone, so whoever was trying to reach him would just have to wait.

Another incoming message sounded.

Heaving an exasperated breath, Lexi sat up and grabbed the phone, intending to turn down the volume. But when she saw a woman's name on the caller display screen, she paused.

Jocelyn—whoever she was—had sent pictures to Quentin.

At five-thirty in the morning.

Lexi frowned, an uneasy feeling creeping over her.

Who the hell is Jocelyn?

She gnawed her lip, her gaze shuttling between the bathroom door and the phone in her hand.

Don't do it, her conscience warned. *You know better than anyone that no good can come of snooping through a man's belongings. It only leads to disillusionment and heartache.*

On the other hand, Lexi argued back, *it's better to know the truth—no matter how painful—than to continue living a lie.*

As she'd already learned the hard way, ignorance was *not* bliss.

The phone buzzed again.

With a sinking sensation in the pit of her stomach, Lexi pressed the button to retrieve the first message.

An involuntary gasp escaped her.

It was a picture of a beautiful, dark-skinned woman lounging seductively on a bed. She wore a sultry smile and skimpy red panties, her arms coquettishly crossed over her ample, naked breasts. The text message read: *Want to see the rest? Give me a call, Counselor.*

Lexi clicked off the picture with trembling fingers and swallowed the bile that had risen in her throat.

Why are you so upset? her conscience demanded. *It's not as if you and Quentin are a couple. Just because you shared one hot, unbelievably spectacular night of lovemaking doesn't mean he's ready to give up his womanizing ways.*

Besides, she thought cynically, some of the best sex she'd ever had with her ex-husband came right after he'd been with his mistress. *Guilt sex,* he'd later confessed to her.

Lexi grimaced. God, she'd been *such* a fool to think that Quentin Reddick could ever change.

"Hey, Lex," he called from the shower. "Sure you don't wanna join me in here? The water's *real* nice and hot."

Her temper flared.

Flinging back the covers, she lunged from the bed,

yanked on her rumpled blouse and skirt, then stalked over to the bathroom.

Inside the steamy glass stall, Quentin stood with his eyes closed and his face lifted to the shower spray as water rushed down his naked, glistening muscles. Ignoring the way her belly clenched, she snatched open the door.

When Quentin glanced around in surprise, she said with stinging sweetness, "*I* wouldn't care to join you, but I'm sure Jocelyn would jump at the chance. Why don't you ask *her?*"

Quentin frowned, blinking water from his long lashes. "Who?"

"Jocelyn," Lexi spat, shoving the cell phone up to his face.

He took one look at the provocative photo, then closed his eyes and groaned. "Lex, it's not what you—"

"Save it." She spun around and marched back into the bedroom, tossing the phone onto the bed. As she retrieved her discarded bra and panties from the floor, she heard the water shut off. She hurriedly tugged on her underwear and pulled down her skirt just as Quentin strode from the bathroom, a towel haphazardly draped around his hips and water streaming down his chest.

"Listen to me," he said urgently. "I'm not sleeping with that woman—"

"Yet." Lexi smirked, her bra balled up in her fist. "But it's only a matter of time, right? I mean, I know how fast you work. Well, except in my case. It took you a bit longer to get *me* into bed, but hey, good things come to those who wait, right?"

His heavy brows slammed together as he advanced on her. "What the hell are you talking about?"

"Admit it, Quentin," she taunted, backing away from him. "You've always loved a good challenge. And what could be more challenging than getting your best friend of twenty years into bed?"

He stopped short, staring at her incredulously. "You honestly think that's what last night was about?"

Instead of answering that, she demanded, "Who's Jocelyn?"

He scowled. "She's nobody."

Lexi snorted derisively. "She must be *somebody* if she's up at the crack of dawn sending you half-naked pictures of herself."

Quentin started toward her again, the towel sliding precariously lower on his lean hips. "Listen to me—"

"When?"

"When what?"

"*When* did you meet her, Quentin? Before or after you kissed me in Burgundy?"

He hesitated, jaw clenched. "I met her last Wednesday. She's—"

"So that would be *after* we got back from Burgundy, correct?"

"Yeah, but it's not like that. She's one of our new clients—"

"A *client?* That's even worse!"

As Lexi pivoted and strode from the bedroom, Quentin followed her. "Damn it, Lex. If you'd just let me explain—"

"There's nothing to explain," she cut him off. "If you see nothing wrong with sleeping with your clients, that's your business."

"I'm not sleeping with her!" he roared.

"Well, she seems pretty confident that you will be soon enough. And if she's just a client, why the hell is she calling your personal cell phone? Explain that!"

Quentin was hot on her heels as she hurried down the

staircase and headed toward the foyer. Her trench coat, shoes and pantyhose lay in a bundle near the front door, taunting her with memories of last night.

As she jammed her feet into her stilettos, she muttered caustically, "I don't even know why I'm surprised. I mean, the morning after you kissed me, I saw that supermodel slinking out of your damn room."

Quentin frowned. "You saw her?"

"Sure did. I was on my way to your room to walk you downstairs for breakfast. Before I could even reach the door, Giselle came strutting out in a sexy little dress."

"Nothing happened," Quentin insisted. "She sneaked into my room that morning—"

"Sneaked?" Lexi repeated skeptically.

"Yes," he snapped. "We weren't staying at a hotel, so I didn't think to lock my door when I went to bed. Anyway, she was waiting for me when I came out of the bathroom. I politely told her I wasn't interested and sent her on her way."

"Staring at her ass until she was out of sight," Lexi jeered.

He scowled. "I wanted to make sure she really left."

"Whatever." Lexi shoved her arms into her coat, working hard not to stare at a bead of water that trickled down his chiseled six-pack and disappeared beneath the waistband of his towel. *Note to self: next time you have an argument with a gorgeous hunk, make sure he's fully clothed!*

As Quentin reached for her, she batted his hand away and snatched her purse off the foyer table.

He sighed harshly. "Don't leave like this, Lex. Let's talk—"

"There's nothing to talk about." She glared at him. "No sane woman would send a man risqué photos of herself unless he gave her the impression that such photos would be welcomed *and* appreciated. So at the very least you must have flirted with her. Which wouldn't be so bad if she weren't your client, and if you hadn't kissed *me* the day before and told me that you couldn't stop thinking about me!"

"That wasn't a lie," Quentin growled. "I *can't* stop thinking about you, damn it."

"Riiight. I notice you didn't refute the part about flirting with that woman and leading her on." She shook her head in angry disgust. "You're so predictable, Quentin."

As she spun toward the front door he grabbed her arm. She tried to twist out of his grasp, but he was too strong. Thinking fast, she snatched off his towel and hurled it across the room, as far as she could throw it.

Cursing a blue streak, Quentin released her and went to retrieve the towel, giving her an opportunity to make her escape.

By the time he recovered and came after her, she was already at the elevator.

"Lexi!" he called, striding purposefully down the corridor. "Wait, damn it!"

One of his neighbors emerged from his condo, took one look at Quentin in his bath towel and arched an amused brow.

Lexi jumped into the elevator and quickly stabbed the down button. As the doors began to close, she heard the man joke, "You must be losing your touch, Reddick."

Scowling, Quentin gave him the finger and stalked back to his penthouse.

Chapter 11

That evening, Lexi sat in a plush leather booth tucked into a private corner of Wolf's Soul. A plate of crab-stuffed mushrooms and an apple martini sat before her, mostly untouched. She had no appetite.

"Lexi?"

She glanced up. At the sight of the young, good-looking man standing at her table, she smiled. Her first real smile in hours. "Hi, Byron. How are you?"

"I'm good." Byron Devers smiled, flashing dimples that made him look even younger than his twenty-six years. "Mind if I join you?"

She did, actually. She was in no mood for small talk. But Byron looked so eager that she would have felt like an ogre if she'd refused him.

"Sure. I'd love some company."

He slid into the opposite side of the booth. "You've

hardly touched your mushrooms. Is something wrong with them?"

"Not at all. They're delicious." She gave him a teasing smile. "So you don't have to send them back to the kitchen for me."

He grinned. "I was just about to offer. I guess old habits die hard."

"Yep."

Up until two years ago, Byron had been a waiter at the restaurant, a gig he'd had since high school. Michael and Quentin had taken him under their wing, encouraging him to attend Morehouse, their alma mater. He'd worked nights at Wolf's Soul to help pay for his tuition. When he'd graduated from law school the year before, Quentin had gotten him a job at Marcus's law firm. Byron was a good kid. Sweet, smart and adorable to boot.

Smiling, Lexi reached for a crab-stuffed mushroom. "So, how do you enjoy being an associate?"

He beamed. "It's great. I'm learning so much, and of course the pay is phenomenal. I'm making way more than any of my classmates from law school who got jobs at other firms."

Lexi chuckled. "It's nice to work for one of the top firms in the country, isn't it?"

"Heck, yeah. But the caseload and long hours definitely take some getting used to," he admitted.

"I'm sure." She gave him a sympathetic smile. "Hang in there."

He grinned ruefully. "I don't have much of a choice. Quentin's a slave driver."

"Hmm." Noncommittal, she nibbled on her mushroom.

"It was great seeing you at the trial yesterday. You left before I had a chance to say hello."

Lexi had been so focused on Quentin that she'd almost forgotten Byron was there. "Yeah, I had to get back to campus to teach a class."

He nodded, surveying the paperwork spread out on the table. "So what're you working on?"

"A proposal for my next cookbook. Being here at the restaurant always inspires me. And if Michael's around, I like to bounce ideas off him."

Byron smiled. "Your first cookbook comes out soon, right?"

"Yep." *Vive la Soul* contained an eclectic fusion of French cuisine and soul food recipes, Lexi's signature as a chef. "Anyway, my next proposal is due to my editor next week."

Byron took the subtle hint. "I won't hold you up," he quickly assured her. "I stopped by for a quick dinner and was just about to leave when I saw you sitting here. I thought I'd come over and say hello."

"I'm glad you did," Lexi said warmly. "It's always good to see you, Byron."

He blushed. "You were always one of my favorite customers," he told her with a shy smile. "You were never rude or demanding. And you gave the best tips."

Lexi was touched. "That's very sweet of you to say, Byron. Like you, I waited tables to put myself through college, so I know what a thankless job it can be." She winked at him. "We waiters have to stick together."

He grinned. "Most definitely."

As she sipped her martini, Byron lingered, making no move to leave. She sensed that he had something on his mind, so she waited.

Finally he blurted, "Would you like to have dinner with me on Thursday night?"

Lexi stared at him, thinking she'd heard wrong. "Are you asking me out on a date, Byron?"

He swallowed, his Adam's apple bobbing in his throat. "Uh, yes. I am."

Lexi set down her glass slowly, wondering why she was so surprised. Michael and Quentin had always teased her about Byron having a crush on her, but she'd never given it much thought. He was like a kid brother to her. Dating him would make her feel like a cougar.

He was watching her carefully. "I've caught you off guard."

"Completely." She chuckled. "I don't know what to say, Byron."

"How about yes?" he suggested hopefully.

She gave him a gentle smile. "I'm very flattered, but—"

"Thursday is jazz night at the restaurant. We could have dinner, enjoy some good music. It'll be fun."

"I know. I always enjoy jazz night, and I'm sure we'd have a good time. But I'm afraid I'll have to pass."

He looked crestfallen. "Do you mind if I ask why?"

"For starters, Byron, I'm too old for you."

He frowned. "No, you're not. You're only—"

"Don't." She held up a hand. "Never announce a woman's age. Not to her face anyway."

"Sorry." He grinned sheepishly, rubbing the back of his neck. "Guess I still have a lot to learn about women."

Lexi smiled, touched by the note of self-deprecation in his voice. He was so sweet, so quaintly innocent. She thought of Quentin, whom she'd also known since he was eighteen. He'd always exuded confidence and charisma, an innate magnetism that had belied his youth. He'd had a swagger long before the word was popularized.

Stop thinking about him, she silently ordered herself.

You've already expended enough emotional energy on that man. Enough is enough!

"Lexi?"

She blinked at Byron. "Did you say something?"

"Yeah." He hesitated. "I asked if there's anything I can say to convince you to have dinner with me."

"Hmm." She pretended to consider him, cataloguing his clean-cut good looks, dimpled smile, smooth brown skin and warm chocolate eyes. His designer suit accentuated his lean build, and she remembered, from his days as a waiter, that he had a cute tush. He *definitely* had potential if she'd been on the prowl for a boy toy. Which she wasn't.

But maybe you should be, a little voice enticed.

This Friday marked what would have been her four-year wedding anniversary, a day that was bound to be difficult for her. Maybe a date with Byron was what she needed. A pleasant distraction to help take her mind off her problems—namely, Quentin.

But she couldn't use Byron like that. It wasn't fair to him. "You should be going out with someone your own age," she told him. "A handsome, successful guy like you? I bet you have to beat the girls off with a stick."

He shrugged dispassionately. "I'm not really interested in any of them."

I'm interested in you. The words hung between them as clearly as if they'd been spoken.

Lexi sighed. "Truthfully, Byron, I'm in a…weird place right now. I'm not sure I'd be very good company."

He gazed at her. "This ten-minute conversation I've had with you has been the best conversation I've had all day."

"Oh, kiddo." She laid her hand over her heart. "You're really sweet, know that?"

"That's what I've been told." He flashed another one of those shy, boyish smiles.

And she sighed in resignation. "All right. Pick me up at six."

On Wednesday night, Quentin drove home a hero.

He'd just won one of the biggest cases of his legal career.

After a speedy deliberation, the jury had found in favor of his client, awarding him $2.8 million dollars in compensatory and punitive damages. The hefty settlement was a repudiation of the defendant as well as the entire health-insurance industry.

Since that morning, news of the verdict had been splashed all over the cable news channels. Quentin had been contacted by reporters from around the country and had received an outpouring of support from perfect strangers, who'd flooded his inbox with emails. He was scheduled to appear on *Larry King Live* and *Good Morning America* on Monday.

At the office, Marcus had broken out Cuban cigars and champagne, and made an effusive toast that had Quentin's ears burning with embarrassment while his colleagues laughed and ribbed him.

Old girlfriends and lovers had been blowing up his cell phone all day, coyly offering to help him celebrate his victory in proper fashion.

Yeah, he was everybody's hero today.

Except the one person whose opinion mattered the most.

For the past two days, Lexi had been ignoring his phone calls. At first he'd been annoyed. Then incredulous. Then dejected. By the time he'd left her a blistering fourth message, he was deadly furious.

Payback's a bitch, ain't it, Mr. Love 'Em and Leave 'Em?

Quentin scowled as he maneuvered through the busy downtown streets by rote.

He couldn't believe Lexi was punishing him for a crime he hadn't even committed. Since their argument, he'd found himself replaying his consultation meeting with Jocelyn Savoy. He'd analyzed every word spoken, every gesture made, to see whether he'd inadvertently given the woman mixed signals. She was beautiful, no doubt. And he'd often been accused of flirting without conscious thought, like his brain was naturally programmed to do it. Hell, he'd flirted with Reese the first time he met her, and still did so every now and then just to get a rise out of Michael. But it was harmless. He had no desire whatsoever to make a play for his best friend's wife, and he damn sure wasn't stupid enough to sleep with a client.

So *had* he flirted with Jocelyn Savoy? Maybe a little. He'd still been smarting from Lexi's rejection the night before, so maybe he'd turned up the charm with Jocelyn to make himself feel better. But he definitely hadn't said or done anything overt enough to warrant receiving topless photos from her, damn it. After Lexi stormed out on him, he'd called Jocelyn and told her that if she *ever* pulled another stunt like that, she'd find herself looking for another attorney. And just for good measure, he'd reassigned her case to one of the firm's senior associates so he wouldn't have any dealings with her.

When it came to his prior bad acts regarding women, Quentin knew the evidence was seriously stacked against him. But after everything he and Lexi had shared, how could she think he'd jump from her arms into another woman's bed? And how could she believe he'd only wanted her because she presented a challenge? Didn't she know how much she meant to him?

The night they'd spent together had been pure, unadulterated heaven. Really, the experience couldn't be accurately described without the accompaniment of a celestial choir.

Quentin had slept with countless women, had experienced every sexual position known to man and had probably even invented a few of his own.

Nothing, *absolutely nothing,* could have prepared him for making love to Lexi.

She'd rocked his world.

When she'd showed up unexpectedly at his place that night, the sight of her had nearly brought him to his knees in worshipful gratitude. He'd been obsessing over her for days, despite his attempts to remain solely focused on the trial. When she'd first arrived at the restaurant for dinner, he'd taken one look at her in those scandalously sexy stilettos and he'd wanted to devour her whole. Who knew that his sweet, feisty little sidekick could inspire such powerful lust in him? Who knew that she could wring such mind-blowing orgasms out of him?

Of course he'd always been aware that Lexi was no virgin. Over the years they'd swapped stories about their relationships and had sought each other's advice on dealing with the opposite sex. So, yeah, he knew she was getting laid—and how often. But whenever he'd envisioned her sleeping with other guys, he'd slammed the brakes on his thoughts, reminding himself that she was his best friend, therefore he had no business speculating about her sex life. Oddly enough, this had been harder to remember when she was married. Every time he'd imagined Adam McNamara running his hands all over her, kissing her and making love to her, some dark, unnamed emotion had stirred within him.

Once, when McNamara was supposed to be out of town

on business, Quentin had gone over to the house to watch a basketball game with Lexi. She'd answered the door with mussed hair, flushed cheeks and kiss-swollen lips, sheepishly explaining to him that her husband had come home early from his trip.

Quentin had stayed away for a month.

But he no longer had to keep his distance from her. Even if he'd wanted to, he couldn't. He'd tasted paradise, and he had to have more. There wasn't an inch of Lexi's beautiful body that he hadn't kissed or caressed in his determination to stake a claim on her. Because make no mistake about it. She belonged to him now. And there wasn't a damn thing she could do about it.

His silent cell phone mocked him, wrenching a savage curse from his mouth.

Instead of being on top of the world tonight, basking in the glow of his courtroom victory, he felt like tearing something apart with his bare hands.

As soon as he got home, he changed into sweats, tugged on a pair of his father's old boxing gloves and headed to his weight room to take out his frustration on the punching bag. As classic Motown songs of redemption and heartbreak played in the background—courtesy of his dad's old record collection—Quentin jabbed and punched the bag as if he were fighting a despised opponent in the boxing ring.

By the time Smokey began crooning "The Tracks of My Tears," Quentin had worked up a good lather. He pulled off the gloves and stalked to the kitchen to get some water.

A surprise awaited him inside the refrigerator.

An expensive bottle of Jameson Rarest Vintage Reserve—his favorite Irish whiskey.

With a slow, delighted smile spreading across his face, Quentin removed the bottle and read the attached note dictated in Lexi's neat, looping script: *Congratulations,*

Q. I'm so proud of you. Here's a toast to my favorite crusader.

His gaze skipped further down the card. *P.S. But I'm still not speaking to you.*

He scowled, then stared up at the ceiling and shook his head in resignation.

She giveth, and she taketh away.

Chapter 12

Wolf's Soul was crowded by the time Lexi and Byron arrived on Thursday evening. Nearly every table and booth was occupied. Smooth, pulsing jazz performed by the Howlin' Good band added to the lively din of laughter, conversation and clinking glasses that permeated the restaurant.

Surveying the crowd from the doorway, Byron grinned. "I usually miss working here. Not tonight, though."

Lexi chuckled. "I don't blame you."

"Michael said he'd save us a table close to the stage." Byron held out his arm to her. "Shall we?"

Smiling, Lexi tucked her arm through his, and together they advanced into the deep, plush cave of the restaurant. As she scanned the faces in the crowd, she instinctively braced herself for the moment she'd see Quentin.

It didn't take long.

He was seated at a table near the stage with a group of

men. The "Morehouse Nine," as the friends were dubbed back in college, had remained thick as thieves over the years. They held season tickets to Atlanta Falcons games and got together every month for a boys' night out.

Quentin was leaning back in his chair with an air of lazy self-indulgence, a toothpick dangling from a corner of his mouth as he nursed a glass of—what else?—whiskey. He was arrestingly masculine in a charcoal dress shirt with the sleeves rolled up to his forearms and the top three buttons undone. As Lexi watched, he made a joke that drew a round of raucous laughter from his friends. The sight of his irreverent white grin disarmed her, causing a deep ache of longing to wash over her. Despite the fact that she'd spent the past three days ignoring his phone calls, she missed Quentin. She missed being with him, talking to him, laughing with him. She wished they could go back to the way things used to be. But it was too late, and that saddened her. Deeply.

As if sensing the weight of her stare, Quentin glanced up suddenly, those piercing hazel eyes locking on to hers. Her breath caught in her throat. Something soft flickered in his eyes, disappearing a moment later when his gaze shot to Byron at her side. His expression hardened before he glanced away, coldly dismissing them.

But Byron had already spotted him. "Oh, hey, there's Quentin," he said, pointing excitedly. "Let's go say hello."

Lexi inwardly groaned. Greeting Quentin was the *last* thing she wanted to do, at least not until she'd knocked back a few drinks to calm her nerves. But there was no way for her to refuse without arousing Byron's curiosity.

So she plastered on a bright smile and allowed herself to be led over to Quentin's table. But as they drew closer, Byron spied one of his former law school classmates and made a detour to greet him, telling Lexi he'd catch up to her shortly.

As she approached Quentin's table, she was met by a chorus of rowdy male voices and wolf whistles. "Hey, Sexy Lexi!" the men greeted her with the nickname they'd bestowed upon her years ago.

She grinned, tossing her bangs out of her eyes. "Evening, fellas." Her gaze swept around the table, briefly meeting Quentin's before passing on. "You boys staying out of trouble?"

"Depends on your definition of trouble," one of the friends slyly intimated, which set off the usual round of deep laughter. Only Quentin remained silent, watching Lexi with a coolly veiled expression as he drank his whiskey.

"Damn, Lexi," said Percy Sheldon, looking her over with frank male appreciation. "You are *smokin'* hot tonight."

There were nods and hearty echoes of agreement around the table.

"Why, thank you, fellas," Lexi drawled, smiling demurely. "I do believe the handsomest men in this restaurant are sitting right here at this table."

It was true, she realized. The eight black men gathered around the table could have been easily featured in *Essence* magazine's annual bachelor issue. They were smart, successful, physically fit, with looks ranging from attractive to downright gorgeous. It was no wonder nearly every female eye in the restaurant was trained on their table. Surprisingly, only one of the friends was married. Michael—who was currently mixing and mingling with his customers—was the first member of the group to be taken off the market. They had a bet going about which one would get hitched next.

Against her will, Lexi found herself stealing a glance at Quentin. He was still watching her, his gaze sliding over her body as if he could see through her low-cut black dress, through her silk pantyhose and satin lingerie, right down to her naked flesh. It was a bold, deliberately possessive perusal. One intended to brand her, to remind her in no uncertain terms that she belonged to him—whether she'd arrived there with another man or not. It couldn't have been more potent than if he'd run his hands all over her body.

Lexi shivered, heat pulsing through her veins.

"Hey, Lexi," Percy said good-naturedly. "How come you never gave any of us the time of day, but you're here on a date with that schoolboy? Now, you *know* he can't handle a woman like you."

She arched a brow, amused challenge in her eyes. "And you think you can, Percy?"

As the others whistled and hooted, Percy grinned broadly. "I sure would love a chance to find out. Matter of fact, why don't you ditch the schoolboy and—ouch!" He whipped his head around to glare at Quentin. "Damn, Q, what the hell'd you kick me for?"

"Did I? My bad," Quentin drawled lazily. "I was just stretching out my legs. Sometimes I forget how far they reach."

Everyone laughed as Percy scowled, leaning down to rub his injured shin.

Lips twitching, Lexi met Quentin's gaze. The possessive gleam was back, letting her know that he'd kicked his friend on purpose, and would probably do worse if she continued flirting with him. Apparently, *he* was the only one allowed to flirt with others, Lexi thought sourly.

"Hey, guys," Byron said, joining them.

A chorus of greetings went around the table.

Byron grinned at Quentin. "Hey, boss. Always great to see you outside of the office."

Quentin inclined his head briefly.

Percy said to Byron, "The fellas and I were just wondering how you convinced Lexi to go out with you."

A huge, goofy smile swept across Byron's face as he gazed at Lexi. "Believe me, I know how lucky I am."

Lexi smiled at him. "We should go claim our table before someone else does." Slipping her arm through his, she said to her friends, "Enjoy your evening, fellas."

"You kids don't stay out too late," Quentin warned softly. "Byron's got a busy day at work tomorrow."

Byron grinned, gave a mock salute. "Yes, sir."

As they moved off, Lexi could feel the searing heat of Quentin's gaze boring into her, compelling her to glance back. But she resisted the urge. She knew the only way she'd be able to enjoy the evening was to put him out of her mind, starting now.

But this proved to be easier said than done, she soon discovered. Because even if she'd been able to pretend that Quentin wasn't seated a few tables away, it wouldn't have mattered. Byron couldn't stop talking—correction, *gushing*—about him.

"...honestly don't know how I could have gotten through law school without Quentin. He really took me under his wing, making sure I understood the course material and kept my grades up. And since he'd also gone to Emory, he was able to give me advice on how to deal with certain professors. He's been great. I couldn't have asked for a better mentor."

"I'm sure," Lexi murmured, taking a languid sip of wine. "Maybe you'd like to go sit with him. He's probably a better date than me too."

As her teasing words registered, an embarrassed flush crawled up Byron's neck, and he groaned. "God, I am *so* sorry, Lexi. I can't believe I've been sitting here going on and on about my boss. You must think I'm such a loser."

"Not a loser," she said with an indulgent smile. "You just have a slight case of hero worship."

"Slight?" Byron grimaced ruefully.

"It's understandable." Lexi paused, then added quietly, "Quentin and I have been friends for a very long time. Believe me, I know what a wonderful, generous guy he is."

Which is why you're trying to shut him out of your life, right?

She shook the troubling thought from her mind and smiled gently at Byron. "You don't have to worry about filling every lull in our conversation. Just relax and be yourself."

"Okay." He smiled shyly at her. *Such a cutie pie.* "I'm really glad you're here with me, Lexi."

"Me too." She ignored a pang of guilt at the reminder that she'd only gone on the date to take her mind off Quentin.

Joke's on you, her conscience mocked.

As the band struck up another set, Byron grinned teasingly and scooted his chair closer to hers. "I'd better start putting those pointers to good use."

Lexi arched a brow at him. "Pointers?"

He looked sheepish. "I was so nervous about tonight that I went to an expert for dating advice. Without divulging your name, of course."

"What expert?" But she needn't have asked.

"Quentin."

Lexi sighed. It was going to be a *long* night.

Chapter 13

Quentin was still seething with fury the next morning when he stalked past his secretary's desk.

"Good morning, Mr. Reddick," she greeted him cheerfully.

"Morning," he growled, because there was nothing "good" about it. "Has Byron come in yet?"

"Not yet, sir."

"When he gets here, tell him to come see me."

"Yes, sir. Would you like some coffee?"

"Not right now, thanks."

He strode into his plush corner office suite—an upgrade Marcus had insisted upon when Quentin became joint owner last year.

Ignoring the broad expanse of windows that overlooked downtown Atlanta, Quentin dropped heavily into the chair behind his desk, scrubbed his hands over his face and tried to remember how many glasses of whiskey he'd imbibed last night to block out torturous mental images of Lexi and Byron writhing all over her bed. The new bed, which had replaced the one tainted by her ex-husband and his mistresses.

"Rough night?"

Quentin glanced up to find Marcus leaning in the open doorway with one shoulder propped on the doorjamb, hands tucked into his pockets. In no mood to be interrogated by another Wolf brother, Quentin grunted unintelligibly and reached for his phone to check his voice mail.

"I had to push our meeting up to ten-thirty," Marcus informed him. "I'm going to be out for a few hours this afternoon."

"Fine."

Instead of leaving, Marcus entered the office and wandered over to the wall of windows. As he gazed out at the downtown skyline, the expression on his face reminded Quentin of a kid who was bursting to share a secret.

Reluctantly intrigued, Quentin set down the phone receiver. "What's on your mind, Lit—Marcus?" He automatically checked himself before he called him "Little Man," the nickname he and Michael had given Marcus when they were younger because he'd always tagged along after them, trying to hang with the big boys. Quentin made a point of not using the nickname when he and Marcus were at the office, but every so often it slipped out.

Marcus turned from the window, beaming from ear to ear. "Samara's pregnant."

"Really?" Quentin grinned broadly. "Hey, man, that's wonderful news. Congratulations."

"Thanks. I suspected something was up when we were in France and she threw up after we went fishing. She said the smell of the fish bothered her, but I remembered how sick she got when she was pregnant with the boys."

"Have you told the family?"

"Not yet. Samara wants to wait until after Mike and Reese have their baby. She says they deserve to enjoy their time in the spotlight, just like we did."

"Thoughtful woman, that wife of yours."

"Always." Marcus smiled softly. "We have a doctor's appointment this afternoon. We're hoping it's a girl this time. Not that we'll know for a few months."

"Are you going to find out?" Quentin asked. "Or are you going to wait like Mike and Reese?"

"We want to know. Definitely. But either way, it's all good." Marcus looked happy enough to float away at any moment.

Quentin was surprised to feel a sharp pang of envy. Did he want what Marcus had? A doting wife, adorable kids, a big, beautiful house in Buckhead? Was he *truly* ready to give up his bachelor pad, wipe his PDA clean of women's phone numbers and become domesticated?

Seeing his frown, Marcus gave him a knowing, sympathetic grin. "Lexi still not speaking to you?"

"No." Quentin's eyes narrowed. "How the hell do you know about that?"

Marcus chuckled. "You must have called her while she and Samara were out running errands for the baby shower. Samara says Lexi took one look at caller ID, saw your number and shut the phone off."

Quentin scowled. "Don't tell your brother. I don't feel like hearing his damn mouth."

"Your secret's safe with me. But just out of curiosity, what'd you do this time?"

"For once," Quentin grumbled morosely, "not a damn thing."

Marcus gave him a long, assessing look. "I believe you."

"Gee, thanks, Wolf."

"No, I'm serious. I know what it's like to be presumed guilty until proven innocent, and it's no picnic." He paused, his expression turning thoughtful. "You know, Lexi reminds me a lot of Samara."

"In what way?"

"Tough, headstrong, vulnerable. They both went through a lot with their mothers. And they both have daddy issues, which, unfortunately, makes it hard for them to trust the men who genuinely care about them."

Marcus wasn't saying anything Quentin didn't already know. But considering that Marcus had successfully weathered the storm and gained Samara's love and trust, Quentin figured the man probably knew what he was talking about.

"So what's your advice, Confucius?"

Marcus smiled cryptically. "Don't get caught kissing any supermodels."

Remembering Lexi's accusations about Giselle, Quentin swore colorfully under his breath.

Marcus laughed. "See you at ten-thirty."

Shortly after he'd left the office, Byron stuck his head through the doorway. "You wanted to see me, boss?"

"Yeah." Quentin waved him inside.

As soon as Byron sat in one of the leather visitor chairs across from his desk, Quentin said without preamble, "When you asked me for dating advice yesterday, I didn't know you were going out with Lexi."

Byron flushed. "I was trying to be discreet. I know you guys are best friends. I wasn't sure if she'd want you to know that, uh, we were, ah—"

Impatient, Quentin cut him off. "No more dates with Lexi. Got that?"

Byron looked confused. "I—I don't understand."

"Look—" The lawyer in Quentin reminded him to tread with caution. Byron was his employee, and this was a personal matter. He couldn't give him the impression that there'd be some sort of workplace retaliation if the kid didn't comply with his demand.

Quentin knew all that—but he didn't give a damn. "All you need to know is that Lexi is off-limits. I like you, kid, but if you insist on seeing her again, you and I are gonna have a serious problem. Feel me?"

Stunned, Byron gaped at him for several moments, then swallowed hard and nodded.

"Good." Quentin smiled, leaning back in his chair to defuse some of the tension between them. "Whatever happened to that cute little hairstylist you were seeing a while ago?"

"Diamond?" Byron made a face. "Didn't work out. Besides, she's nothing like—" He broke off, but Quentin knew what he'd been about to say. *She's nothing like Lexi.*

He wondered if he, too, would forever judge other women by that standard.

"Lexi and I had a good time last night." Byron smiled wryly. "That is, after I got rid of my butterflies."

Quentin narrowed his eyes. "Define 'good time.'"

Byron met his gaze, correctly interpreted what he was asking and let out a nervous little laugh. "That's kind of a personal question, boss."

Quentin was already measuring the width of the massive desk, mentally calculating whether it'd be quicker to go over it or around it to get his hands on his young associate.

Seeing the leashed violence in his eyes, Byron got quickly to his feet. "If we're done here, I, uh, have some client phone calls to make."

"Go," Quentin snarled, a dismissal and a warning.

Temper simmering, he shoved to his feet and paced to the windows.

Pausing at the door, Byron said tentatively, "There's just one thing. What am I supposed to do about tonight?"

"Tonight?"

"Yeah. I'm, uh, supposed to see Lexi again. She was going to make dinner for me."

The words slashed through Quentin's heart like the blade of a well-honed dagger. He turned his head with eerie slowness and stared at Byron. "What did you just say?" he asked in a chillingly soft voice.

Byron visibly gulped. "Lexi offered to cook dinner for me."

Red swam before Quentin's eyes.

A moment later he was storming across the room with an expression of such lethal fury that Byron actually cowered against the door. As Quentin stalked past him, he growled, "I suggest you make other dinner plans, kid, or you're gonna starve."

Chapter 14

When Lexi glanced up from the menu she'd been finalizing and saw Quentin bearing down on her, an analogy of a raging bull was the first thing that came to mind.

She froze, her mouth drying to dust and her knees quaking as she stared at him.

Really, who *wouldn't* have trembled at the sight of a six-foot-five, two-hundred-forty-pound man with bright, flashing eyes and a positively ferocious expression charging toward them? She'd never seen Quentin so furious. So she did what any sane, self-respecting person in her shoes would have done: she turned and fled.

"Yeah, you'd better run," came his growled taunt behind her.

Her options, of course, were woefully limited. The only escape route was the swinging door through which Quentin had just erupted. So she ducked inside the large kitchen pantry. She realized her mistake at the same time Quentin laughed darkly and muttered, "That's even better."

He followed her into the pantry and yanked the door closed behind them. As Lexi retreated from him, he stalked her step for step until he'd backed her up against the wall, successfully trapping her.

Fighting to ignore the erratic pounding of her heart, she stared up at him. "Wh-what're you doing here, Quentin? I have class in twenty minutes."

Planting his hands on either side of her head, he lowered his face to hers until she could see that his irises were, fittingly, as dark and ominous as storm clouds. The heat from his body scorched her, spiking her own temperature until she thought they'd both burst into flames. When her students came looking for her, all they'd find was a pile of smoldering ashes.

"How long are you going to keep fighting what's between us?" Quentin spoke in a deceptively soft voice that belied the dangerous tension radiating from his body.

Lexi swallowed convulsively. "I'm not fight—"

"Wrong answer. Try again."

Her temper flared. "How can you say I'm fighting? I slept with you—"

"That's right. You did. And it was absolutely amazing. But the next day you got cold feet. So you cut and ran."

"I did not! That woman kept texting—"

"Bullshit!" Quentin roared, slamming his fist on the wall beside her head and making her jump. "I've already told you nothing happened between us. And you know that's the truth. But even if she hadn't sent those pictures, you would've found a reason to bail that morning. Because deep down inside you're afraid to believe that maybe, *just maybe,* this thing between us is real."

"No. *No.*" Lexi shook her head, even as his words

reached into the deepest corners of her soul and threatened to expose her darkest secrets and fears. "Don't try to turn the tables on me. I have every reason to have doubts about you, Quentin, and you know it."

"What I know," he growled savagely, "is that I'm crazy about you. I want to be with you, damn it, and I'm gonna do everything in my power to make it happen."

Lexi squeezed her eyes shut. She was trembling uncontrollably, a potent combination of anger, adrenaline, fear and arousal speeding through her veins. "This isn't a good time, Quentin," she said in a shaky voice. "I'm at *work*."

"Yeah? Well, you shoulda thought about that before you decided to stop taking my damn calls."

A heartbeat later his mouth was grinding against hers. She inhaled sharply as a wave of pleasure crashed through her. Her hands slid up his chest and curved around his neck as if they had a mind of their own. She could feel the hard bulge of his erection pressed against her belly, an unholy temptation.

He lifted her off the floor, grabbing her legs and drawing them around his waist. Even as she mentally cursed her decision to wear a skirt to work that day, her body quivered at the brush of his fingers dragging the material up to her hips, pushing it out of the way. When he reached between her thighs and discovered that she wore a thong, he crooned in wicked satisfaction.

"Mmm." He nudged aside the damp strip of silk. "You must have known I was coming for you today, Alexis."

She shivered and groaned as he stroked the slick, swollen lips that sheathed her clitoris. "You're trying to get me fired," she whimpered.

"And *you're* trying to get me disbarred and sent to prison."

"Am not!" she choked out as he slid a long finger inside her.

"Are too. When Byron told me you were cooking for him tonight, I almost lost my damn mind. Are you trying to get that boy killed?" he demanded, his fierce, glittering gaze sweeping across her face as he eased a second finger into her. "Do you know what it did to me when I thought of you cooking for another man?"

"It's just dinner," Lexi countered weakly.

"Wrong," he snarled. "It's more than dinner. It's about you sharing yourself with him the way you do with me. It's *never* just about the food, and you damn well know it."

She did. Heaven help her, she did. And maybe that was why she'd offered to cook for Byron. Some small, perverse part of her had wanted to spite Quentin. And now he'd come to mete out her punishment.

He kissed her roughly and possessively, his tongue sliding in and out of her mouth in time to his thrusting fingers. A wave of contractions rippled through her belly. Beneath her starched chef's jacket, her breasts throbbed and her nipples had grown painfully hard. She was burning everywhere, helpless against the onslaught of her desire. A desire unlike anything she'd ever imagined or experienced before.

Removing his fingers from her body, Quentin reached down and unzipped his pants.

Lexi gasped, realizing, too late, that she'd let things go too far. "Quentin, no! Not here! My students—"

His expression darkened. "I don't want you cooking for any other man."

Raw need stabbed through her groin as he rubbed the thick head of his penis against her engorged clitoris, his precome mingling erotically with the wetness that coated her sex. "Do you understand me? Say you won't ever do that again."

Even as ecstasy beckoned on the horizon, Lexi balked at the possessive command. "Quentin—"

Without warning he drove into her, wrenching a broken cry from her throat. *"Say it."*

"I won't cook for any other man," she sobbed out helplessly.

He flashed a dark, feral smile. "Good."

His slow, deep thrusts sent tremors of sensation tearing down her spine, convulsing her womb. As she moaned, his hands caressed her hips and curved underneath to grasp her butt, kneading and massaging.

"You have no idea the hell you put me through last night," he uttered in a low, rasping voice. "Or maybe you do. Strolling into the restaurant on another man's arm. Wearing that sexy as *hell* dress. Forcing me to sit there and do nothing while my friends undressed you with their eyes. You had to know what you were doing to me. You had to know how much it killed me to watch you and Byron together the whole night."

Lexi could only groan, her world centered on the single exquisite spot where their bodies were joined. Each deep, gliding thrust intensified the burning ache between her thighs, driving her toward that cataclysmic release only *he* could give her.

Leaning down, he nuzzled the side of her throat, finding the sensitive hollow beneath her ear that made her shiver. "Promise me you won't see Byron again."

She clung to his upper arms, feeling the thick muscles bunch and flex as his strokes deepened, lifting her up and down against the wall.

"Promise me."

Shuddering, she panted, "I promise."

But he wasn't finished with his demands.

Cradling her face between his hands, he feathered a line of slow, soft kisses from her forehead to her mouth, his intense hazel eyes boring into hers. "Give me a chance to prove to you that I'm ready for a relationship, Lex. No walls, no barriers, no ghosts from the past. Just you and me."

Her heart raced, and she had to struggle to answer. Could she really trust him? Was she ready to stop running, as he'd accused her of doing? Was she ready to take the plunge and fly with him? And if they crashed and burned, would she lose his friendship forever?

"Quentin, I—"

Just then the first batch of her students arrived, the sound of their laughter and voices echoing around the large, industrial kitchen.

Lexi's eyes flew wide. Seized by panic, she stared up at Quentin. The wicked amusement in his eyes only heightened her alarm. He had her at his complete mercy, and he knew it. If her students caught her having sex in the pantry, she'd not only lose her job; she could pretty much forget about teaching at any other respectable culinary school.

Watching her face, Quentin slid out of her with excruciating slowness, stopping just at the tip. A scream rose in her throat, threatening to explode from her lips.

"Say yes," he whispered.

Yes! she mouthed desperately.

He brought his cheek next to hers, sucking her earlobe, murmuring at her ear, "What was that, sweetness? I couldn't hear you."

Ruthless cad!

"Yes," she hissed into his ear.

A slow, satisfied smile curved his mouth.

"I have to go," she whispered frantically, circling her hips against his, begging him to finish what he'd started.

He shook his head. "Not yet."

Holding her gaze, he eased all the way back into her, inch by inch, so that she could feel the slow slide of her juices as her body sheathed him. She nearly came right then, and had to bite her lip hard to suppress a mewling cry of ecstasy.

Eyes glinting devilishly, Quentin began thrusting into her as more voices entered the kitchen. Lexi grabbed his taut, round butt, urging him to go harder and faster. Thankfully, he was so aroused that he cooperated. Soon their coupling grew frenzied, both fueled by the knowledge that they could be discovered at any moment.

When Quentin finally whispered, *"Now,"* Lexi's inner muscles tightened around him, clenching and spasming as pleasure tore through her.

Quentin slanted his mouth over hers, smothering the wild cry she'd been unable to hold back. A moment later he shuddered deeply, coming in a rush of scalding heat that flooded her womb. Locked together, chests heaving, bodies trembling, they stared at each other.

From outside the door, one of the students speculated, "Maybe we're not supposed to be in the kitchen today."

"I could have sworn we were," another voice spoke up. "But maybe not. The holiday break's still throwing us off."

"Let's go see if she's in the classroom."

Lexi held her breath, waiting to see if any stragglers would remain behind. When the room grew mercifully silent, she exhaled a deep sigh of relief and whispered a prayer of undying gratitude.

Chuckling softly, Quentin gave her a quick kiss, then

unwrapped her legs from his waist and set her back down on the floor.

As they hurriedly fixed their clothes, Lexi shot him a dark glance. "I am *so* gonna kill you for this," she hissed.

"Why? You didn't get caught."

"I could have!"

"But you didn't." He grinned. "It's a sign."

"Of what?"

"That we're meant to be together."

She scowled, yanking down her chef's jacket. "Because we didn't get caught having sex at my workplace?"

"Exactly." His eyes glimmered with mischief. "It also means we can make this a new Friday ritual."

"I don't think so!"

Quentin laughed, dark and wicked.

Without conscious thought Lexi reached up to straighten his silk tie. He ran a hand over her hair, smoothing down the disheveled strands as he smiled into her eyes. "What time is dinner tonight?"

Her lips twitched. "Don't push your luck."

Grabbing his hand, she tugged him toward the door. She opened it a crack and peeked out just to make sure the coast was really clear. Seeing the empty kitchen, she crept out of the pantry with Quentin in tow.

"Now get out of here before my students come back," she told him, trying to shoo him out the door.

He didn't budge.

"What now, Quentin?" she whined in exasperation.

"You didn't answer my question."

"About what?"

"Dinner."

She heaved a resigned sigh. "Fine. Be at my house at seven."

Leaning down, he captured her lips in a deep, lingering kiss that liquefied her bones. As she sighed and swayed into him, he drew back and winked at her. "I'll be there at six."

And then he turned and sauntered out the door, whistling so cheerfully that Lexi could only shake her head and laugh.

Chapter 15

That night, sated from a lavish dinner and two hours of passionate lovemaking, Lexi and Quentin lay spooned together under a blanket on the living room floor. A cozy fire crackled in the hearth, and soft, romantic ballads serenaded them from the CD player.

Lexi had made coq au vin and opened a bottle of wine. Instead of eating in the formal dining room, they'd headed to the living room and spread a big, thick quilt across the floor. And then they'd fed each other, sharing kisses between bites and sipping from the same glass.

Wrapped in Quentin's strong arms, cocooned in heat and steel, Lexi thought she could get *very* used to nights like this.

"What're you thinking about?" Quentin murmured, nuzzling the nape of her neck.

She sighed, a soft, dreamy sigh. "Fate."

"Fate?"

"Mmm-hmm. I wasn't even supposed to be at that party the night we met. I had planned to go home for the weekend."

"Really? I never knew that."

She grimaced. "I got into a heated argument on the phone with my mother. So I decided not to go home after all. But my friends had already left for the party, so I didn't have a ride. I could have caught the bus, but I didn't have the address of the party. So I'd resigned myself to spending a miserable Friday night alone."

Quentin's cheek was now resting gently against hers. "So what happened?"

"I stepped out of my dorm room to get a snack, and that's when I ran into some girls who were heading out to the party. I had a class with one of them, so she kindly offered to let me catch a ride with them if I hurried up and got ready." Lexi smiled softly. "So just think. If I hadn't argued with my mother, stayed on campus and run into those girls, I wouldn't have gone to the party. Which means I wouldn't have met you that night. Possibly never."

A stillness settled over Quentin. "That," he said quietly, "would have been unthinkable."

She closed her eyes. "I know."

Silence lapsed between them, both marveling at the simple twist of fate that had brought them into each other's lives.

After a few moments, Quentin kissed her cheek and murmured huskily, "Let's go into the bedroom."

Her mouth went dry. "In a little while."

He dragged his lips to her bare shoulder, nipping her gently. "I'd rather go now."

She felt his heavy erection thickening against her butt, felt an answering tug of arousal between her thighs. But she wasn't ready to go into the bedroom yet. She wasn't ready to face the demons that haunted her, especially on this day.

Quentin had grown still again. "Lex—"

She sat up abruptly, dislodging the blanket. "While we're taking a stroll down memory lane, you're not going to *believe* what I came across the other day when I was cleaning out my closet."

Propping himself up on one elbow, Quentin watched as she padded quickly to the entertainment center and knelt down to retrieve an old videocassette. She popped it into the VCR/DVD combo and pressed fast forward until she reached the desired starting point, which she'd memorized years ago.

As she grabbed the remote control and rejoined Quentin on the blanket, he gave her a darkly amused glance that told her he knew she was stalling for time. She wondered if he knew why.

Shoving aside the uneasy thought, she grinned broadly at him. "You're gonna get *such* a kick out of this."

"Hmm," was his noncommittal response.

She hit play.

The television screen was filled with an image of several cloaked figures huddled around a circle. The eerie, haunting strains of gothic music could be heard playing in the background.

Recognizing the footage from an old college step show, Quentin groaned in amused disbelief.

Lexi grinned. "Shh! Here comes the best part."

As they watched, the cloaked specters suddenly dropped to a crouch, revealing two tall, familiar figures in the middle of the circle. They stood back to back, their black hoods drawn menacingly low over their faces.

The sinister organ music abruptly segued to a pulsing drum solo. With military precision, the hooded cloaks were ripped off, and Quentin and Michael exploded into an electrifying step number that had their muscled chests gleaming and hips undulating in a fierce, primal rhythm that made every female in the crowd scream like fans at a rock concert. Lexi knew—she'd been one of them.

Even now, she couldn't help fanning herself as she whistled and cheered at the television.

At the first note of "Atomic Dog," the other members of the group launched into the routine with a synchronized series of stomps, kicks and hand claps that brought the audience to its feet with a roar of approval.

As the performance ended, Lexi clapped loudly and whooped with delight while Quentin chuckled and shook his head.

"Those were the days," she fondly reminisced. "Man, you and Mike had some *serious* moves!"

"Had?" Quentin pretended to be affronted.

She rolled her eyes at him in laughing exasperation. "Don't worry, baby. You can still work it." She winked. "And not just on a stage either."

"That's better," he grumbled, lips quirking at the corners.

Not only were Quentin and Michael the best dancers; they'd also been the best-looking members of their fraternity. So they'd often been used to kick off the group's performances.

"You and Mike were *so* exploited," Lexi teased.

Quentin chuckled. "We didn't exactly mind."

"I guess not, considering you two got all the ladies."

Quentin flashed a cocky grin and flexed his arm, the tattooed bicep bulging impressively. "Recognize."

"What!" Lexi grabbed the throw pillow she'd been lying on and smacked him upside the head with it. "Recognize *this!*"

Laughing, Quentin wrestled her to the floor and pinned her beneath his big, heavy body. She giggled, squirming and bucking her hips in a comically futile attempt to dislodge him. When she saw the wicked intent in his eyes, she shook her head in desperate entreaty.

"Oh, no. Please not that. I beg of y—" Her plea choked off into a squeal as Quentin dug his fingertips into the secret spot between her ribs that he'd discovered years ago.

As he tickled her, Lexi shrieked with hysterical laughter, her head rocking back and forth against the blanket.

"Not so big and bad now, huh?" Quentin taunted. "All I gotta do is find your kryptonite."

"Q," she gasped, laughing so hard that tears ran from the corners of her eyes, "please...*stop!*"

He grinned. "Naw. You need to be taught a lesson, woman."

"Please!"

"Uh-uh."

"You're gonna make me wet myself!"

Those marauding fingers paused. "Well, now, considering that we're *both* naked, that might not be such a good thing."

Lexi's next howl of laughter joined his as he relented, wrapping his arms around her and rolling over so that she was on top. She clung to his neck, gasping and trying to catch her breath.

Gradually she became aware of his hot, rigid erection prodding her belly. His hands stroked down her back, then cupped the swell of her bottom. As currents of sensation flooded her loins, she sighed and murmured without thinking, "This is the kind of scenario Adam always thought he'd walk in on."

Instantly she knew it had been the wrong thing to say.

Quentin's body locked up like he'd been tasered with a stun gun.

When she raised her head to look down at him, his eyes cut straight through her like the laser-driven scope of a rifle.

"What the hell did you just say?" he demanded.

Lexi swallowed hard. Wordlessly she rolled off him and sat up, pulling the blanket over her body. Her nudity suddenly felt uncomfortable. Too revealing.

"I'm sorry," she mumbled, staring at Quentin as he propped himself up on one elbow and snapped the other edge of the blanket over his waist. "I shouldn't have said anything."

"Too late." His voice was flat. Hard. "Now repeat it so I can make sure my ears weren't deceiving me."

She drew a long, shaky breath. "I never told you this, though maybe you could sense it, but Adam hated our friendship. *Hated it.* He felt threatened by our closeness, and sometimes it made him lash out in cruel ways."

Quentin stared at her, looking as if the blood had suddenly drained from his head. "Did he ever—"

"No, he never hit me. That wasn't really his style," she said, bitterly mocking. "He was more into psychological abuse."

Quentin's eyes narrowed. "What do you mean?"

Lexi squeezed her own eyes shut, as if by doing so, she could block out the painful memories. "If I wore a certain blouse or skirt, he'd sneer at me and ask me if I was going to see you that day. When you came over one time while he was supposed to be on a business trip, he swore up and down that we were having an affair. And sometimes when we made love he'd taunt me, accusing me of wanting you in our bed instead of him, asking me if you were a better lover and if you had a bigger 'jackhammer,' as he crudely put it. He made me feel so dirty when he talked like that, and *not* in a good way." She shuddered convulsively.

Quentin was deadly silent.

"Honestly, it's a miracle I didn't let him poison our friendship," she continued grimly. "I think that's what he wanted. And I think it gave him some sort of sadistic pleasure to bring women into our bed. It's like he was getting even with me for something he thought I'd done, or wanted to do." Her mouth twisted cynically. "In the end, when I demanded a divorce, he had the nerve to claim that my friendship with you drove him to cheat. *That's* when I really knew how depraved he was."

"Son of a bitch." The words exploded through gritted teeth. *"Son of a bitch!"*

Wearily Lexi held up a hand. "It's all right—"

"The hell it is!" Quentin roared, his face contorted with fury. "That bastard was *never* good enough for you, and I knew it the moment I met him! But I held my tongue because I saw how much it hurt you every time your mother criticized him. For two years I kept my distance from you as much as possible because I never wanted to give him any reason to think I was disrespecting his marriage. I missed the *hell* out of you, Lex, but I put your happiness and peace of mind above my own selfish needs. The *only* reason that filthy piece of shit accused you of cheating was to ease his own guilty conscience!"

By the time he'd finished his furious tirade, Lexi was trembling so hard her teeth chattered. She drew her knees up to her chest and wrapped her arms around her legs, wishing like hell she'd never opened this Pandora's box with Quentin. What had possessed her?

"I need his address." Quentin's voice was low with suppressed rage.

"No." Her answer was swift, unequivocal. "Absolutely not."

"Forget it. I'll find him myself."

"And do what, Quentin?" she cried. "Beat him to a bloody pulp? *Kill* him? And then what? You wanna rot in prison for the rest of your life, or until the State of Georgia puts you down like a rabid dog? Adam McNamara isn't worth it! You hear me? He isn't worth it!"

"That's for me to decide," Quentin snarled.

"No, it isn't! *I'm* the one who was married to him, not you. I've already warned you to stay away from him, but you're so damn hotheaded!"

"It's been two years, and I haven't gone after him *once!*"

"Only because he changed jobs and his phone number and address are unlisted! My God, Red, you've got the man living like he's in the witness protection program. He actually told his lawyer that he feared retaliation from you!" She shook her head in angry disbelief. "I don't need you to defend my honor or fight my battles. Last I checked, *I* kicked *his* sorry ass in divorce court!"

"Not good enough," Quentin bit off.

"It is for me!" Eyes narrowed dangerously, she jabbed a warning finger at him. "I've told you once, and I'm telling you again. If you get yourself locked up, I won't visit you in prison. Not one single day! And I mean it!"

His eyes darkened, nostrils flaring. "That's just a chance I'll have to take."

"Try me."

"Alexis—"

"If you go to prison, you'll kill me, too. Is that what you want?"

He averted his gaze, a muscle pulsing at the base of his tightly clenched jaw.

Silence, raw and volatile, lapsed between them.

When Lexi's nerves were stretched to the breaking point, Quentin said in a low, sullen voice, "I'm sorry."

"Me too," she whispered at once.

"It's hard, you know? Hard to watch your best friend go through hell and you can't do a damn thing about it. You were a wreck for a whole year after the divorce. It killed me, Lex. *Killed* me."

"I know. We shed more than a few tears together." She gave him a wan, grateful smile, remembering how wonderful and attentive he'd been to her during those dark, bleak days when all she'd wanted to do was curl up in the fetal position and never leave her bed. Quentin had often left work early and brought over dinner from the restaurant just to make sure she ate. They'd played cards and video games and watched movies together. He'd coaxed smiles out of her when no one else could. And sometimes, when she'd just needed to be held, he'd done that, too. Lexi knew she couldn't have gotten through the painful ordeal without Quentin. He was her Rock of Gibraltar.

She swallowed, drew a deep, shuddering breath and slowly exhaled. "I'm sorry, Quentin. We were having such a good time tonight. I shouldn't have brought up Adam. It's just that… Having you here with me… On my anniversary…" She trailed off, suddenly too embarrassed to continue.

But Quentin reached up and grasped her face between his hands, forcing her to meet the piercing directness of his gaze. "Finish what you were going to say."

She licked her lips. "You're the first man I've slept with since my divorce."

A range of emotions crossed Quentin's face—surprise, tenderness, relief. Gratitude. "You gave me the privilege of being your…first?"

"Yes," she whispered, gazing earnestly at him. "And I wish to God you really *had* been my very first lover."

With an agonized groan Quentin crushed his mouth to hers, kissing her so hungrily and fiercely her head spun. She clung tightly to him as he swept her up into his arms, stood and started purposefully from the living room.

When she realized where he was heading, she panicked. "Quentin, the guest bedroom is—"

"I know where the hell it is," he snarled. "I'm not taking you there. And I'm not a damn guest!"

"But—"

He silenced her with a look that warned her the fun and games were over. This was serious business, and the outcome of this match of wills could change the course of their lives forever.

He strode into the master bedroom with the single-minded determination of a general storming the gates of a fortress. If the door had been closed he would have kicked it open, crashing it against the wall.

Lexi trembled as he gently laid her on the king-size bed and lowered his body over hers. His hot, possessive gaze drilled into hers, stripping away her defenses. Laying her bare.

"I told you," he growled. "No more walls. No more barriers. No more ghosts from the past."

"Quentin—"

"I know what this is about. You've been stonewalling all night, and now I know why. You didn't want to bring me in here because in some warped way, you feel like you really *are* cheating on Adam. Like you're justifying his crazy, jealous accusations by being with me." He pushed his face into hers, scorching her with the feral intensity of his gaze. "But you didn't do anything wrong. Do you hear me? *You* didn't do *anything* wrong!"

He seized her mouth in another deep, mind-blowing kiss that left her reeling. And then he was sliding lower, slowly kissing his way down her trembling body. His lips ignited brushfires everywhere they touched, his hands stroking and exploring her flesh until there was no part of her he hadn't claimed as his own. She was burning with fever, shivering with need. By the time he reached the aching place between her thighs, she was so primed that all it took was one stroke of his tongue against her swollen clit and she arched off the bed like a rocket had gone off inside her.

"That's right," Quentin crooned with dark satisfaction as she convulsed and keened with helpless pleasure. "There's nothing wrong or dirty about what we're doing. Nothing in my life has *felt* more right than making love to you, Lex."

He moved over her, and their lips and tongues met and meshed until they were both breathing harshly. Quentin drew back, pushing himself to his knees. Lexi followed him, her hungry gaze fixated on the long, engorged penis jutting insistently from his body.

Her eyes locked with his as she wrapped her hand around his shaft and eased him into her mouth. He groaned and shuddered convulsively. He was big, the blunt head easily reaching the back of her throat and beyond. His skin was hot, thick and firm, a steel bar drenched in melted chocolate. She slid him in and out of her mouth, working her lips and tongue as she simultaneously massaged his engorged sac. His guttural moans intoxicated her, made her drunk on her own sensual power. And somewhere deep inside her, a naughty, vengeful little voice whispered, *Yes, Adam, he* is *bigger, thank you very much!*

And then Quentin was shuddering and climaxing, his penis pulsing and contracting violently as he exploded inside her mouth. He watched her swallow his seed, his heavy-lidded eyes glittering with fierce adoration.

And she stared back at him, shaken by the profound intimacy of this moment. A moment shared with the one man she was never, ever supposed to want.

Lovingly Quentin stroked her hair. "We can do anything we want, sweetness," he said huskily. *"Anything."*

He lowered his head, slanting his mouth over hers. They shared another kiss. Languorous, achingly slow, lips parting and coming together again. And then he turned her around, keeping her on all fours.

"If I want to take you from behind—" he thrust into her, tearing an animal cry from her throat "—we can do that, too."

Gripping her hips, he began rocking against her, a slow, measured pace that had her moaning and grabbing fistfuls of the bed linens. Sweat soon coated their bodies, making their skin so slick that each thrust echoed in a wet slapping sound. Quentin caressed her butt and cupped her swinging breasts, brushing his thumbs over her tight nipples until her moans grew wilder.

Whispering rough-tender endearments, he leaned over her, embracing her as he kissed between her shoulder blades and nuzzled the nape of her neck. Her skin was so sensitized that the scrape of his bristled jaw sent electric shivers racing to her engorged clit. Before she could reach down, his nimble fingers were already stroking her, soothing the raw ache. She gyrated and ground her hips against his, needing him to go faster. But he maintained his slow, relentless rhythm, every plunge and glide of his hot, silken hardness driving her closer to the edge.

And then, without warning, he pulled out of her and rolled her onto her back. He pushed her legs open, braced himself on his arms and reentered her with one deep thrust, capturing her sobs in his mouth.

Her shaking thighs were spread achingly wide as he began pumping into her, now showing her no mercy as she writhed and arched beneath him. He countered every surge of her hips with heavier strokes, driving her back down into the mattress. Her hands rushed blindly over his flexing back and down to his butt, clamping over the firm, clenching muscles.

This was more than sex. This was soul-shattering, life-altering *lovemaking*.

Poised above her, his face taut with passion as he gazed into her eyes, Quentin commanded, "Say my name."

"Quentin," Lexi whimpered.

"Louder, damn it. Sing it from the rafters. Chase away these damn ghosts."

"Quentin," she sobbed.

"Louder." He pulled back and thrust deep. "Louder!"

"Quentin!" she screamed as her body exploded in an orgasm of such cataclysmic proportions she swore she wouldn't—*couldn't*—survive it.

A moment later Quentin erupted. With his head thrown back, the sinewy cords of his neck straining and his powerful body bucking, he shouted *her* name in a hoarse, rapturous voice that brought tears to her eyes.

As the waves of ecstasy crashed over her, breaking her down and liberating her, she clung tightly to him and wept with sweet, glorious abandon.

Quentin gathered her protectively into his arms, cradling her head against his chest and holding her like he'd never let go. "I love you," he whispered fervently. "I love you so damn much I can't *breathe* without you."

Her heart soared, and an unspeakable joy blazed through

her. She gazed into his eyes through a sheen of tears and whispered, "I love you too, Quentin."

And deep inside her heart, buried so deep she'd been afraid to go anywhere near it, another truth echoed. *I always have.*

Chapter 16

"Ma? Where y'at?"

"In here, baby."

Munching on a juicy apple he'd swiped from the kitchen, Quentin followed the sound of his mother's voice to the sunroom located at the rear of her house. She was humming softly as she folded linen napkins and placed them around a table set with her best china and crystal. A centerpiece of fresh-cut flowers from her garden perfumed the air.

"Howdy," Quentin said around a mouthful of apple.

"Hey, June bug. How are—" She glanced up. And froze. "Lord have mercy," she breathed, looking as if she'd seen a ghost.

Quentin would have glanced over his shoulder to check for an apparition hovering behind him, but he knew the ghost his mother saw was reflected in his own face.

After several moments, Georgina Reddick blinked to clear her vision and let out a shaky laugh. "I'm sorry, baby.

Goodness gracious. You look more and more like your daddy every day. It catches me by surprise sometimes."

Quentin smiled quietly. "I know."

She gazed at him a moment longer, then shook her head as if to banish the memories of her late husband, a police officer who'd been killed in the line of duty when Quentin was thirteen.

As she resumed folding napkins, Quentin sauntered over and leaned down to kiss her upturned cheek. Draping an arm around her shoulders, he surveyed the elegant place settings on the table. "Your turn to host the monthly book-club luncheon?"

"Sure is." She sent him a sly smile. "The ladies will be happy to see you. You know how much they enjoy showing you photos of their daughters and nieces, hoping you might take a shine to one of them."

At the thought of being ambushed by his mother's matchmaking friends, Quentin grimaced. "What time do they get here?"

"Two o'clock."

"I'll be gone by one."

Georgina laughed.

At sixty-three she was as beautiful as she'd ever been in her youth. With her smooth honey complexion, patrician features and luminous smile, she bore such a striking resemblance to the actress Lonette McKee that strangers often stopped her on the street and asked for her autograph, which tickled her to no end.

Quentin crunched into his apple. "Need help setting the table?"

"No, thank you. I'm almost finished." She poked him playfully in the ribs. "You don't know the proper way to fold napkins anyway."

He grinned. "Didn't seem like a skill I'd need in order to practice law."

She laughed. "Go on with you, boy."

Chuckling, Quentin wandered across the sun-drenched room, which was surrounded by walls of glass and overlooked a lushly manicured backyard. It was his mother's favorite room in the elegant Victorian house he'd bought for her when he made partner at his old law firm. Although he knew he could never repay her for all she'd done for him, that had never stopped him from lavishing expensive gifts on her.

Georgina came from a proud old Southern family who'd disinherited her when she married Quentin's father—a brash young amateur boxer from the wrong side of the tracks. After Quentin was born, Fraser Reddick had traded in his boxing gloves for a badge and a steady paycheck. But he'd never forgotten his first love. Quentin's fondest childhood memories included trips to the gym with his father, who'd taken him into the ring and taught him how to box. The first victim of Quentin's vicious left hook was a neighborhood bully who'd made the mistake of calling him a pretty boy. That offense, coupled with a lewd slur about Quentin's mother, had landed the tyrant in the emergency room. Furious and appalled by his violent behavior, Georgina had grounded Quentin for a month and forbade his father from giving him any more boxing lessons. But whenever her back was turned, Fraser had winked at Quentin and whispered proudly, "How's my champ doing? Man, what a bruiser!"

Quentin smiled now at the memory. God, he missed his father. Although Sterling Wolf had become like a surrogate dad to him over the years, no one could ever fill the void left by Fraser Reddick. Which was probably why Quentin's mother had never remarried. She'd loved Fraser so much that she'd defied her powerful family and forfeited her inheritance to be with him. Even after he died, she hadn't gone crawling back to her parents to beg their forgiveness. Instead she'd channeled her grief into raising Quentin and making sure that he never lacked for anything. Georgina was the epitome of a steel magnolia.

"So, June bug, I didn't expect to see you until Reese's baby shower this evening."

Pulled out of his reverie, Quentin turned from the window. "I know. I figured I'd surprise you."

Georgina glanced up from arranging silverware on the table. "You did surprise me. Made my day, too."

They traded affectionate smiles.

As Quentin walked over and discarded his apple core in a plastic trash bag filled with cut flower stems, his mother asked, "How's Alexis?"

"She's good." He smiled softly. "We're good."

"We?" Pausing in her task, Georgina arched a finely sculpted brow. "Is there something you want to tell me?"

As Quentin grinned at her, he realized how much he'd looked forward to confiding in her. "Lexi and I are dating, Ma."

She went still. "Is that so?"

He nodded, all but bouncing on his heels.

"Well." A slow, pleased smile spread across Georgina's face. "It's about time."

Quentin stared at her in surprise. "What do you mean?"

"I've been wondering how long it would take you to wake up and realize you're in love with that girl."

"What?" Quentin exclaimed, startled. "No, Ma, you don't understand. This just happened. While we were in France."

Georgina smiled, shaking her head slowly at him.

"Precious heart, you've been in love with Alexis for years."

"Years!" Incredulous, he barked out a laugh. "Quit playing, Ma."

"I'm not."

"What in the world makes you think I've been in love with Lexi for *years?*"

An intuitive gleam filled Georgina's dark eyes. "A mother knows these things." At his skeptical look, she sighed. "Okay. Since you're a lawyer, I'll support my case with evidence. Exhibit A? The way you look at Alexis. The way your eyes light up whenever you talk about her. The way you can't help touching her, even for the briefest moments."

Quentin swallowed. "Circumstantial. Those examples don't prove anything."

"All right, Counselor. How about this example? When Alexis got married four years ago, you took it *very* hard."

Quentin clenched his jaw, every muscle in his body going rigid.

His mother's expression gentled. "I watched you during the wedding ceremony. You looked positively tortured, sweetheart. When the minister asked if anyone objected to the marriage, I swore you'd be on your feet and charging down that aisle faster than I could say 'Lord have mercy.' And you weren't very sociable at the reception either. Alexis had to practically beg you to dance with her. And the look on your face as you held her? Oh, baby, it just about broke my heart. And what did you do after the reception? You drove to Michael's restaurant, sat alone at the bar and got drunk. Not drunk from too much celebrating. No, you got lick-your-wounds drunk. The bartender had to fetch Michael to drive you home, you were so incapacitated."

She paused, arching a brow. "Strange behavior from someone whose best friend had just gotten married, don't you think?"

Quentin scowled, even as his chest tightened. "I knew she was making a big mistake by marrying that loser. And, yeah, I was a little sad that our friendship wouldn't be the same."

"Are you sure those are the only reasons you were so upset?"

He held his mother's quiet gaze a moment longer before his eyes slid away. Shaken and dumbfounded, he scrubbed a hand over his face and blew out a deep, ragged breath. Was it possible? Had he been in love with Lexi for years and not even known it? Or had he been in denial about his feelings?

"Do you know why you've had such a hard time settling down?" his mother gently prodded.

He sent her an ironic glance. "I haven't exactly been trying."

She smiled, soft and knowing. "That's because you've been secretly holding out for Alexis. No other woman will do."

Quentin said nothing.

His mother's words had struck a chord deep within him, unearthing truths he'd been unable—or unwilling—to acknowledge until now. Her description of his behavior at Lexi's wedding was frighteningly accurate. He *had* been miserable that day, starting from the moment he'd sneaked into the bridal suite and seen Lexi standing in front of the mirror, outrageously beautiful in her simple white wedding gown. He'd wanted a private moment with her, but her mother and bridesmaids had shooed him out of the room, fussing that the bride had to finish getting ready. Later, as Lexi wafted down the aisle toward her groom, she'd sought

Quentin out among the gathered guests. When their eyes met, she'd smiled softly and winked. And something inside him had shriveled up and died.

Over the years, he'd often wondered what he would have said to her if they'd been left alone before the ceremony.

Now, in a moment of stunning clarity, he realized that he'd intended to beg her not to go through with marrying McNamara.

Shaken by the revelation, Quentin searched his mother's face. "Is that why you never said anything to me? You wanted me to figure it out on my own?"

She nodded, eyes twinkling. "I knew you would eventually. You're a smart man."

He smiled ruefully. "Not smart enough, obviously, if it took me all these years to see what was right in front of me."

Georgina chuckled. "Better late than never."

"That's true." But Quentin was thinking about how much precious time had been wasted. If he'd recognized his feelings sooner, could he have claimed Lexi before Adam McNamara did? Could he have saved her from the pain and heartache of an emotionally abusive marriage? He'd never know, and that saddened him thoroughly.

His mother was watching him with a quiet, nostalgic expression. "You know, your daddy was quite the ladies' man when we met. So dashing and daring, and so charismatic. He could charm the skin off a snake, and no woman could resist him. Sound like anyone you know?"

At Quentin's sheepish grin, she laughed and gave him a knowing look.

Sobering after a moment, she continued, "When your father married me, none of those other women mattered. For the sixteen years I had him, that man never once cheated on me. And I never worried that he would. Because he loved me." She reached up and tenderly cupped Quentin's cheek. "That's the kind of love you have for Alexis. A rare, profoundly special love that only comes around once in a lifetime."

Quentin swallowed, surprised to feel moisture pricking his eyelids. "I don't want to lose her," he confessed, husky with emotion.

Georgina's gaze softened. "Then don't," she said simply.

And Quentin vowed, right then and there, that he wouldn't.

Chapter 17

The next two weeks were heaven on earth.

Lexi and Quentin spent every possible minute together, which was no easy feat considering their busy, demanding careers. But they found creative ways to make it work. When Quentin flew to New York to appear on *Larry King Live* and *Good Morning America,* Lexi canceled her classes for the day and went with him, rationalizing that she could kill two birds with one stone by having lunch with her editor while she was in town.

Once she and Quentin had concluded their business for the day, they locked themselves in their luxurious suite at the Waldorf-Astoria, ordered room service and devoured each other for the rest of the night.

They spent countless hours in bed together, alternately making passionate love and talking, rediscovering little things about each other that amused and fascinated them. They made up trivia questions to test their knowledge of each other. Neither was surprised when they both passed with flying colors.

One weekend they tackled the job of repainting Lexi's family room, which she'd been wanting to do since the divorce. She'd never really cared for the color Adam had chosen, but she'd capitulated to keep the peace. Now, as she worked alongside Quentin, she found it incredibly cathartic to cover the walls with a fresh coat of terra-cotta-colored paint.

Out with the old, she thought. *In with the new.*

When she met Quentin's gaze, she knew he felt the same way.

They had nearly finished their task when Quentin suddenly flicked a spatter of paint at her, hitting her squarely in the chest. After she recovered from her shocked indignation, she'd dunked her own brush in the pan and gone after him. Their laughter rang out as they chased each other around the room, taunting and slinging paint at each other. By the time they were through, their hair and clothes were smeared with paint, and the protective cloth draped across the floor was covered with terra-cotta-colored footprints.

Later, as they cuddled in bed together, Lexi realized that in less than two weeks, Quentin had brought more joy and laughter into her house than she'd experienced in the two years she'd lived there with her ex-husband.

Near the end of the month, Michael invited Lexi to join him and Reese on *Howlin' Good* to promote her cookbook. Halfway through the taping, she was explaining how to prepare one of the featured recipes when Reese abruptly rose from the chair she'd been sitting on.

Michael and Lexi stared at her. "Are you okay?" they asked in unison.

"I'm fine." Reese wore an oddly serene smile. "My water just broke."

"What!" Michael exclaimed, rushing to her side as a wave of excited murmurs swept across the studio audience. "We have to get you to the hospital!"

"I know." Reese's calm smile never wavered as he began ushering her from the set. "But isn't there something you should do first?"

Michael eyed her frantically.

Reese sighed, then grinned into the camera and blithely announced, "In light of the fact that I'm going into labor… that's a wrap, folks!"

Several hours later, Lexi and Quentin entered the quiet hospital room where Reese reclined in the bed, a tiny bundle cradled lovingly in her arms. Michael sat close beside her, as close as he could get without being in the bed with her. Both were beaming with joyous wonder as they gazed upon their newborn daughter's sleeping face, so enthralled that they didn't notice their friends' arrival until Lexi and Quentin had nearly reached the bed.

"Congratulations," they chorused softly, so as to not wake the baby.

The proud parents glanced up at them, both wearing identical rapturous grins. "Hey, you two."

"Hey, yourselves." Lexi and Quentin huddled around the bed to get their first look at the sleeping infant in Reese's arms. Savannah Wolf had inherited her parents' exquisite mahogany complexion and had a head full of curly black hair.

"Oh, my God," Lexi breathed. "She's beautiful."

Quentin grinned. "She definitely takes after her mother."

Michael chuckled. "Nice try, wise guy. But I happen to agree with you."

Laughing, Quentin clapped his friend warmly on the back and handed him a Cuban cigar. "You done good, Daddy."

"Daddy." Michael looked dazed. "Wow. I can't believe I'm a daddy."

Reese gave him a teasing smile. "You'll believe it when you're getting up for two a.m. feedings and diaper changes."

Everyone laughed.

Lexi added a floral arrangement to an already teeming assortment of bouquets, balloons, teddy bears, chocolates and other gifts that had been brought to the new parents. Then, perching on the edge of the bed, she smiled gently at Reese. "Hey, Mommy. And how're *you* feeling after eight hours of labor?"

"Wonderful." Reese sighed, gazing down at her daughter. "Seven pounds, twelve ounces wonderful."

Michael tenderly stroked his wife's cheek. "You were amazing, sweetheart. And I can't believe how composed you were when your water broke. *You* had to calm me and Lexi down."

"I know." Lexi laughed, remembering the mad scramble to get Reese to Emory University Hospital, where she also worked. Her colleagues were going to spoil her rotten during her stay.

She grinned at Michael and Lexi. "Haven't I been telling you guys for months that I know what I'm doing?"

"Yes, ma'am," they humbly conceded, and Reese and Quentin chuckled.

Lexi grinned wryly at Michael. "Your producer must be on cloud nine. I remember how ecstatic he was when you proposed to Reese on the show last year. He *still* hasn't stopped gushing about how your ratings skyrocketed after that episode aired. Just imagine how viewers will respond to Reese going into labor on the show. I smell another Emmy," she added in a singsong voice.

Reese and Michael traded smiles. "In that case," she said, "we'll have to keep coming up with milestones to celebrate on the air."

Quentin grinned. "Savannah's first step, Savannah's first tooth…"

Everyone laughed.

"Where's the family?" Lexi asked curiously. "Quentin and I thought we'd have to fight our way into the room when we got here."

Reese grinned. "Michael shooed everyone out so I could feed the baby. I think they all headed back to Dad's house for a celebration dinner."

"The whole gang was here?"

"Yep," Reese replied. "My parents and Raina and Warrick. Dad and Asha. Mom and Grant flew in from Minnesota. Marcus and Samara brought the boys, who are *very* excited about their new cousin and can't wait to play with her."

Lexi thought of Samara's secret pregnancy and hid a smile. Soon enough, Matthew and Malcolm Wolf would have another playmate to get excited about.

"I'm glad you're both here," Reese said to Lexi and Quentin. "Michael and I would like to ask a very special favor of you."

Michael smiled at them. "We want you to be Savannah's godparents."

Quentin grinned broadly. Lexi gasped, so touched that tears sprang to her eyes. She and Quentin looked at each other, joined hands, then turned back to their friends and chorused, "We'd be honored."

Michael and Reese beamed with pleasure. "Good."

Lexi sniffled. "I need a tissue."

She'd barely gotten out the words before Quentin removed a handkerchief from his pocket, knelt in front of her and gently dabbed at her watery eyes.

"Look at our feisty, tough-talking Lexi getting all sentimental," Michael teased. "What have you done to her, Q?"

Quentin smiled into her eyes. "What has *she* done to me?" he murmured.

Lexi reached out and touched his face before she remembered that they had an audience. She glanced up in time to see Michael and Reese exchange quiet, knowing smiles.

Flushing self-consciously, Lexi grinned at Reese. "May I please hold my precious goddaughter who upstaged me on her daddy's show this morning?"

The others laughed as Reese gingerly handed over the baby. As Lexi cradled the warm, swaddled infant in her arms, something melted inside her.

"Hello, Savannah," she cooed softly. "What a beautiful name for a beautiful little angel. You're going to have your daddy wrapped around your finger. Mommy too." To her delight, the sleeping newborn puckered her tiny lips. "Oh, guys, look—"

Lexi glanced up and froze, arrested by the tender expression on Quentin's face as he stared at her with the baby. When their eyes met, a deep ache of longing swept through her, squeezing her heart almost painfully.

Glancing away, she kissed Savannah's silky crown of curls, then gently passed her to Michael. "Here, Daddy. It's your turn."

As Michael and Reese resumed cooing over their daughter, Lexi and Quentin smiled softly at each other.

They left shortly afterward, promising to return the next day with the rest of the family.

* * *

On the ride home they were unusually quiet, each absorbed in their own private thoughts. When they reached Quentin's high-rise, where they'd already agreed to spend the night together, they rode the elevator to the twentieth floor in silence.

Once inside the darkened penthouse, they removed their coats and hung them up in the foyer closet.

Their eyes met.

Without a word passing between them, Lexi took Quentin's hand and led him upstairs to his bedroom. They undressed each other slowly, then fell across the bed in a tangle of limbs. Moonlight poured through the wall of windows, cascading over them as they rolled around, mouths searching, hands caressing and exploring each other's bodies as if they hadn't already memorized every detail.

Rising over him, Lexi pushed Quentin down to the bed and straddled him. Gripping the thick base of his shaft, she positioned him and sank down. She heard his breath escape in a slow hiss, heard her own moan as her inner muscles tightened around his penis. He steadied her hips with his hands as she began to move on him. Finding a rhythm, she let her head fall back and surrendered to her body's instincts, rocking, riding up and down his length with long, deep strokes. He groaned and fondled her breasts, arching his hips to meet every downward pump of hers.

They came together, shuddering and crying out each other's names. Lexi's heart soared as Quentin spent himself inside her, spurting liquid heat into her womb with violent pulses.

As their gazes locked, Lexi wondered if she was the only one who hoped they'd just created a new life.

Chapter 18

"What an amazing turnout!"

Lexi glanced up at the heavyset, middle-aged woman who had appeared at her table as the last customer left, armed with an autographed copy of Lexi's debut cookbook.

"I think it went pretty well," Lexi agreed.

"Pretty well?" the bookstore manager echoed incredulously. "You had a line wrapped around the corner and you sold out in an hour!"

Lexi smiled, undeniably pleased by the successful outcome of her book signing. Yesterday's event, the first of her two-week book tour, had gone just as well. Not only that, but her cookbook had debuted on a major bestseller list and was already headed for a second printing, according to her editor.

As if those weren't reasons enough to celebrate, she was in love. Deeply, madly in love with a wonderful man who also happened to be her best friend in the world. For the first time in years, Lexi could honestly say that life was good.

"Can I get you anything, Ms. Austin?" the bookstore manager asked, eager to accommodate. "More Perrier? Hors d'oeuvres?"

Lexi smiled, rising from the table. "No, thank you. I'm meeting some friends for lunch—"

"The ones who were here earlier with cameras and big signs?"

Lexi chuckled. "Yes. And one of them is pregnant," she said, referencing Samara, "so I'd better not keep her waiting much longer." She shook the woman's hand. "Thanks so much for your hospitality."

"Thank *you*. It was a real pleasure to meet you, Ms. Austin. I wish you the best with your cookbook."

"Thank you! I appreciate that."

As Lexi headed from the large chain bookstore, she pulled out her cell phone and felt a pang of disappointment when she saw that there were no missed calls. She'd hoped to hear from Quentin by now. After attending her book signing yesterday, he'd left for Washington, D.C., to tend to some business matters at the law firm's other office. Since becoming Marcus's partner, he'd had to take on even more responsibility, which meant more travel. He'd be gone for a week, and Lexi honestly didn't know how she'd make it that long without him. Last night she'd slept in one of his T-shirts, which was so big on her it could have been a muumuu. She'd buried her face in it, inhaling the wonderful, familiar scent that clung to the fabric.

Smiling, she sent him a text message. *I miss you.*

"Alexis?"

She glanced up. A man had appeared directly in her path. Medium height and build, with stooped shoulders and deep lines carved into his pockmarked brown skin. Sunken cheeks and bloodshot eyes rimmed with heavy bags hinted at a life of hard drinking.

As recognition dawned, the ground tilted beneath Lexi's feet and she staggered back a step, staring in shock.

It can't be.

But she knew it was.

Ray Austin. Her long-lost father.

"How ya doing, baby girl?" he said, greeting her as though they'd just spoken the week before. "Looks like I'm too late for your book signing. Real sorry about that. I'd hoped to—"

"What are you doing here?" Lexi whispered, the words forced out through dry lips.

Her father frowned. "I just told you. I came for your book signing. I saw you on TV last week—"

"You saw me," she repeated scornfully. "You haven't *seen* me in over thirty years!"

Ray grimaced. "Well, now, I can explain—"

"You don't need to explain anything. I have no interest in anything you have to say."

He took a step forward and she instinctively retreated, heart knocking painfully against her ribs. Glancing around the busy bookstore, she met the curious stares of several onlookers and realized that she was causing a scene.

"Excuse me." With a curt nod at her father, she sidestepped him and hurried from the bookstore. Once outside, she sucked in deep lungfuls of air. She felt as if she were suffocating, having one of her panic attacks.

Ray followed her out of the store. "I know I haven't been there for you like I shoulda. But—"

She whirled around. "But *what?* All these years without so much as a birthday card or a phone call. And you show up here out of the clear blue, expecting me to—what?

Welcome you with open arms? Call you Daddy?" She raked him with a look of scathing contempt. "You wasted your time coming here."

He had the nerve to scowl. "Don't I have a right to be proud of my daughter's accomplishments?"

"You gave up that right when you walked out on us! And I think we both know that *pride* has nothing to do with why you're here today."

His eyes shifted guiltily from hers.

Lexi felt sick to her stomach. "Just as I thought," she mocked bitterly. "You saw me on TV, and now you think you can weasel your way back into my life to cash in on my newfound success. But you're sadly mistaken. If you think you're getting *one* red cent out of me, think again!"

"Baby girl—"

"Don't you *dare* call me that! I'm not your baby girl. And if you *ever* try to contact me again, I'll take out a restraining order against you. Stay the hell away from me!"

As she spun around and hurried across the parking lot toward her car, he called after her, "Ask your mama why I left. She knows!"

Lexi hurled herself into her car and slammed the door. Her heart was pounding so hard she thought it would explode. She was supposed to meet her friends for lunch, but as she raced out of the parking lot, she had only one destination in mind.

She found her mother sitting in her favorite armchair in the living room, surrounded by a thick, noxious cloud of smoke as she puffed away on a cigarette. On the television, a rerun of *The Golden Girls* blared loudly. As Blanche launched into a spirited discussion of one of her sexual escapades, Carlene cackled and slapped her thigh.

Lexi strode purposefully into the room and shut off the television.

Carlene protested, "Hey, I was watching—"

"We need to talk, Ma." Brimming with fury, Lexi paced up and down the floor.

Her mother watched her for a moment, then took a long drag on her cigarette and shot a stream of smoke from the corner of her mouth. "How'd your book signing go?"

"Great," Lexi snapped. "By the way, so nice of you to show up."

Carlene arched a brow. "Why should I go to your book signing? I don't need an autographed book from you— you're my daughter."

"Exactly! I'm your daughter, and just *once* it would be nice if you could show a little support."

"Is that what's got you so upset? Because I didn't come to your damn book signing?"

"No, Ma," Lexi jeered. "I didn't expect you to come, so how can I be upset that you didn't?"

Carlene's eyes narrowed. "Don't take that tone with—"

"However," Lexi rudely cut her off, "it might interest you to know that while *you* couldn't be bothered to show up, someone else did."

"Who?"

Lexi looked her in the eye. "My father."

She watched as the color slowly leached out of her mother's face. Carlene's hand trembled as she tapped her cigarette into an ashtray on the table beside her, muttering darkly, "What did *he* want?"

"What do you *think,* Ma? He wanted money. He saw me on Michael's show, so he figured he'd come hit me up for cash now that I'm supposedly rich and famous." A nasty, mocking smile twisted her mouth. "Isn't that what he used to do, Ma? Wait until me, Colby and Summer were at school, and then sneak over and hit you up for money?"

Carlene was toking furiously on her cigarette. "You don't know what the hell you're talking about."

"Oh, yes, I do!" Lexi shouted angrily. "I knew every time he'd been at the apartment. The cash in our rainy day jar would be gone, and you were always in an especially foul mood after you'd seen him." She shook her head in grim disgust. "I used to wonder why he never stuck around long enough to see his own children. And I used to wonder why on earth you'd give him money after everything he'd done to you. It was almost like he was blackmailing you."

"You need to leave this alone," Carlene warned in a strained voice.

"Leave *what* alone? The dark secret that's been eating away at you for as long as I can remember? Is *that* what I should leave alone? Well, I can't!"

"Don't you have better things to worry about?" Carlene sneered. "Like keeping that man of yours in check?"

Taken aback, Lexi stared at her. She hadn't told her mother about Quentin because she hadn't wanted to subject herself to a bitter diatribe about cheating men.

"You thought I wouldn't find out?" Carlene taunted, a mocking gleam in her eyes. "Last Sunday in church I overheard Quentin's mama telling the pastor's wife that her prayers had been answered, because Quentin had finally realized he was in love with his best friend from college." Carlene smirked. "Obviously she wasn't talking about Michael, so the only other best friend she could be referring to was *you.* I left before they caught me eavesdropping, but I wouldn't be surprised if they're already planning your damn wedding."

Lexi swallowed hard, but said nothing. She didn't expect her mother to understand the powerful connection she and

Quentin shared. She didn't expect Carlene to admit that maybe, just maybe, Lexi had lucked out and found the real deal: a man who truly loved her and wanted to be with her.

Because deep down inside, her conscience whispered, *you don't completely believe it either. Not yet.*

"I thought you were smarter than that," Carlene muttered, crushing out her cigarette in the ashtray. "After everything Adam put you through, I can't believe you'd be foolish enough to get involved with yet another man who has a wandering eye. I guess some chicks just never learn."

"You're one to talk," Lexi shot back.

When her mother flinched, she felt a stab of guilt.

She should have known the retaliation would be swift.

"I don't know how long you and Quentin have been dating," Carlene said with malicious satisfaction, "but I should tell you that I saw him going into Wolf's Soul with another woman two weeks ago."

Lexi snorted derisively. "Is that the best you can do? Quentin always takes new clients to Wolf's Soul for lunch meetings, male or female. But if he really wanted to sneak around behind my back, do you honestly think he'd be stupid enough to take his mistress to Michael's restaurant, of all places?"

Carlene faltered for a moment, then shrugged. "Maybe he knows Michael would cover for him, the way they did for each other in college. Or maybe he just doesn't give a damn. Rascals like him usually don't. I'm telling you, he and that woman looked *mighty* cozy together."

"I don't believe you." But Lexi hated herself for the kernel of doubt that whispered through her mind, hated the fact that she thought of Jocelyn and her topless photos.

Carlene's eyes narrowed spitefully. "Mark my words. Quentin Reddick's gonna make a damn fool out of you, just like Adam did. And when he does, don't come crying to me, expecting sympathy and support. 'Cause I've tried to warn you that the man's no good, but you refuse to listen! You keep choosing the same type of men—the *wrong* men. And that's why you're never gonna be happy!"

"No! You're wrong!" Lexi shook her head vehemently, resisting the childish urge to clap her hands over her ears to block out her mother's taunting words. "You don't know Quentin the way I do. He loves me. He would never—"

"Ask him," Carlene dared her.

"I'm not asking him anything!" Lexi cried, her voice breaking because she knew her mother might be right about Quentin, and she couldn't bear it.

"What are you so afraid of?" Carlene jeered. "Ask him about that woman he was with!"

"*No!* I won't dignify your ridiculous accusation by repeating it to him. And I know *exactly* what you're doing. You're deflecting, trying to change the subject so I'll forget about my father. But it won't work. I want answers from you, Ma."

Carlene's expression hardened. "You need to go."

"I'm not going anywhere until you answer my questions! My father told me to ask you why he left us. Why did he say that?"

"Your father is a worthless—"

"What is he holding over you?" Lexi roared.

Pushed to the limit, Carlene exploded. "The fact that I almost killed you!"

Stunned, Lexi stared at her, feeling the blood drain from her head.

Several long seconds passed.

"I—I don't understand," Lexi finally managed in a choked whisper.

Carlene lunged to her feet, her face contorted with

anguished rage. "You want to know why you're so afraid of heights? Blame *me!*"

Suddenly Lexi didn't want to hear any more. But she had to know. Had to know the truth once and for all. "What happened?"

Now it was her mother's turn to stalk up and down the floor. "He came home drunk one night, reeking of sex and another woman's perfume. It wasn't the first time, not even close. But I'd finally had enough. You were only two years old. I had my hands full with you, and your father was no help whatsoever. So I'd made up my mind to ask him for a divorce.

"When he stumbled through the door that night, I confronted him about where he'd been and what he'd been doing. He got mad and defensive. We started arguing. Our yelling woke you up. At first I tried to ignore your crying, but you only got louder. Your father started cursing and shouting at me to shut you up. I kept screaming at him to get out, but he refused. Dug in his heels and said he wasn't going anywhere. Something came over me, and I just snapped. I marched into your room and snatched you out of bed. The next thing I knew I was on the patio, dangling you over the railing. We lived on the tenth floor, so…we were up pretty high."

Lexi stared at her in abject horror, nausea and dread churning in her stomach.

"I threatened your father, told him to leave or I'd drop you. He called me a crazy bitch, but he wouldn't get out, wouldn't back down. He was *daring* me to let you go. So I kept dangling you over that railing, and you were kicking your little legs and wailing in terror." Carlene's voice was raw, ravaged with pain and guilt. "Sometimes I close my eyes at night and I can still hear your screams in my head."

Lexi sank weakly onto the sofa, her legs unable to support her.

Carlene continued pacing furiously. "One minute your father was laughing and taunting me. The next minute he was storming across the patio, telling me to stop my foolishness. He grabbed my arm. I tried to shake him off, but he wouldn't let go. And then...and then...*I dropped you!*"

"No!" Lexi screamed, a sound of anguished denial wrenched from the depths of her soul. "No. No. *No!*"

Carlene crumpled to the floor, her body convulsed with the deep, racking howls of a wounded animal.

Reeling, choking with sobs, Lexi descended upon her, thinking she might actually kill her. She grabbed Carlene's frail shoulders and shook her violently as she shouted into her face, "How could you? *How could you?*"

"It was an accident!" Carlene wailed, tears pouring down her cheeks. "I never meant for you to fall!"

"You could have *killed* me!"

"I know. *I know!* It's nothing but the grace of God that kept you alive that night!"

"What happened?" Lexi demanded hoarsely. *"Tell me what happened!"*

Trembling uncontrollably, Carlene squeezed her eyes shut. "One of our neighbors had heard all the commotion. He lived on the ground floor of our building. When he heard you screaming, he stepped out onto his patio and looked up. That's when he saw you dangling in the air. He jumped over his railing and started shouting up at me. When I dropped you—oh, Jesus!—he was there to catch you. By the grace of God, you only came away with a few cuts and bruises!"

"And a paralyzing fear of heights!" Lexi cried shrilly.

"You can survive that! You *couldn't* have survived a fall from ten stories!"

Lexi stared at her mother for an agonized moment, then released her so abruptly that Carlene sagged against the wall.

She shoved to her feet and backed away on rubbery legs, staggered by the enormity of Carlene's horrifying revelations. Were it not for the intervention of a complete stranger, Lexi would be dead. Dead at the hands of her own mother. It was inconceivable.

"I could have gone to jail," Carlene said in a low, haunted voice. "But the neighbor took pity on me and decided not to call the police. Your father promised to change his ways, so I let him stay. But a leopard can't change its spots. He hung around long enough to knock me up two more times before he gave up on the marriage and walked out on us. He moved in with one of his mistresses before she got fed up with him and put his sorry ass out. His drinking eventually got worse, and he fell on hard times. One day he came crawling back to me, begging for money. When I refused to give him any, he threatened to tell you about that night. He said if you ever found out what I'd done, you'd hate me for the rest of your life. So I gave him what he wanted."

"And that's how it started," Lexi said flatly.

Carlene's head snapped up, her features twisted with sudden fury. "I shouldn't have let him blackmail me all those years! I should have let him tell you the truth. What difference would it have made? You grew up to hate me anyway!"

"I don't hate you!" Lexi cried, tears scalding her eyes.

"Well, *I* hate *you!*"

Stunned, Lexi recoiled as if she'd been leveled with a two-by-four.

"Every time I look at you," Carlene spat viciously, "I'm reminded of what happened that night. I'm reminded of the way I allowed your father to push me over the edge, to make me do such an unspeakable thing to my own child. Every time I look at you, I'm reminded of how much I failed you. I can't take any pride or joy in your accomplishments, because I know you achieved them *without* any help from me!"

Lexi gaped at her, torn between compassion and incredulity. "How can you say you didn't help me? You *raised* me—"

"That's right! And I did the best I could! But sometimes, God help me, I wish you hadn't survived that fall. Because if you weren't here, I wouldn't have to be constantly reminded of everything I have *ever* done wrong as a mother. Your father never looked at me the same after that night. He was disgusted with me for dropping you from the balcony. He called me deranged, said I was an unfit mother. He told me the whores he slept with could raise you better than *I* ever could!" She glared accusingly at Lexi. "If only you'd stayed asleep that night. If only you hadn't rattled my nerves so much with all your goddamn wailing! Maybe, *just maybe,* your daddy and I could have worked out our problems. But because of what happened that night—because of *you*—he left us! So yeah, I hate you! *Hate you!*"

Every cruel word lashed at Lexi, battering at her fractured psyche until she finally snapped with an outraged roar, "You know what, Ma? If that's the way you really feel, you don't have to worry about me anymore!"

Carlene went utterly still, staring at her. "What's that supposed to mean?"

"It means I've had enough of you and your toxic bullshit! I'm doing what I should have done a long time ago. I'm leaving Atlanta, and I'm getting as far away from you as possible!"

Panic flared in Carlene's eyes. "You can't do that—"

"Watch me!"

And as Lexi spun blindly and fled from the house, she knew just where she would go.

Chapter 19

Quentin slowed his car to a red light and impatiently drummed his fingers on the steering wheel. He was eager to get to Lexi's house. He hadn't seen her in over a week, and he missed her like crazy.

But that wasn't the only reason for his eagerness that afternoon.

Smiling, he reached inside his breast pocket and removed a small black box. Thumbing the lid open, he examined the four-carat princess-cut diamond ring nestled in velvet. He hoped it wasn't too much. Lexi had never been flashy or materialistic. What moved her more than anything was the sentimentality in simple gestures, like the flowers he'd given her that day in Dijon. Or the romantic dinner he'd arranged to re-create their experience in Burgundy.

Yeah, he knew she wasn't the kind of woman who'd appreciate expensive trinkets he threw her way just because he could afford to do so.

But, damn, he couldn't *wait* to slide this beautiful ring onto her finger.

Assuming she says yes, an inner voice reminded him.

As the traffic light clicked to green, Quentin snapped the box closed and kissed it for good luck.

A few minutes later, he pulled up to the familiar two-story redbrick house and did a double take. There was a For Sale sign in the yard.

He frowned. When had Lexi decided to put her house on the market?

Maybe she's ready to take the next step and move in with you.

Perfect, he thought.

But as he climbed out of the car and walked to the front door, he couldn't shake a sense of foreboding. Because he knew Lexi wouldn't have put her house up for sale without telling him first. Unless she had a specific reason for not telling him.

A reason he wouldn't like.

When she answered the door, he took one look at her drawn face and knew something was wrong.

"Quentin." She gave him a smile that didn't quite reach her eyes. "Welcome home."

He stepped inside the house, swept her up into his arms and kissed her the way he'd been dying to all week. When she responded with equal hunger, he felt some of his misgivings dissolve.

Drawing back, he ran a hand over her soft hair and smiled into her eyes. "I missed you."

"I missed you, too," she whispered, her arms looped tightly around his neck.

"That was the longest week of my damn life."

"Mine too."

He gave her another kiss, then set her back down on the

floor and closed the door behind him. "We have so much to talk about."

"I know." Her voice was subdued. "We hardly spoke on the phone this week."

"I know," he agreed with a grimace. "Between your book-tour schedule and the fires I was putting out at the D.C. office, there just weren't enough hours in the day. I want to hear all about your whirlwind tour. When do you leave for the West Coast?"

"Tomorrow."

Quentin groaned. "So soon?"

"Afraid so."

As they moved into the living room, Quentin claimed his usual spot at one end of the pin-striped sofa. Instead of sitting next to him, Lexi sat on the adjacent mahogany settee.

That set off another warning bell in his head.

He searched her face, noting the faint dark smudges beneath her eyes that indicated she'd been sleeping poorly. "Are you feeling all right?" he asked with gentle concern.

"I'm fine. Just…tired."

Struck by a sudden suspicion—or hope—he stared intently at her. "Are you…pregnant?"

She visibly tensed, a shadow crossing her face. "No. I'm not."

Disappointment crashed through him. Ever since they'd been named godparents of their friends' baby, Quentin had been daydreaming about getting Lexi pregnant. He'd imagined her, lush and petite, waddling around with an adorably swollen belly. And he'd gone further, envisioning her in the kitchen with their daughter, a miniature version of herself, a smudge of flour on their noses as Lexi taught their child how to make one of her divine French dishes.

He would have given anything to walk through her front door and hear the words *we're going to have a baby*. Talk about an unforgettable homecoming.

Reluctantly pushing the thought aside, he focused on the grim, tense woman before him. "What's going on, Lex? Why didn't you tell me you were selling the house?"

Something flickered in her eyes. Something that sent a dagger of fear through his heart. She dropped her gaze to her lap, where her hands were tightly clasped. "I was waiting for you to get back."

"Okay." His voice was remarkably even, considering the awful pressure that had clamped over his chest. "So what's your game plan? You buying another house or…?" He deliberately let the question hang, waiting tautly.

An interminable silence followed.

Finally she lifted guilty eyes to his. "I'm leaving, Quentin."

He felt the bottom drop out of him. Stunned, he stared at her. "Leaving what? Leaving this neighborhood? Leaving DeKalb County? Leaving your job? Leaving *what?*"

"Leaving Atlanta," she whispered.

"The hell you are." His voice was low, feral.

Tears shimmered in those beautiful eyes. "Quentin—"

"What the hell happened?"

She averted her gaze, delicate nostrils flaring as she choked back emotion. "It's not important."

His eyes widened incredulously. "*Not important?* You're talking about leaving Atlanta—*leaving me*—and it's not important?"

"Please don't make this any harder—"

Quick as a shot he was off the sofa and kneeling in front of her, trapping her with his hands on either side of the chair. "What happened?" he growled. "Tell me!"

That broke her. The tears she'd been holding carefully in

check spilled over, and she covered her face with trembling hands. Her anguish cut through Quentin like jagged shards of glass. He pried her resistant hands away and pulled her hard against him, wrapping her tightly in his arms. She buried her face in his chest and wept, releasing a torrent of raw emotions.

He groaned raggedly. "Sweetness, you're killing me. You know what your crying's always done to me."

"I'm sorry," she sobbed against him. "I didn't want to tell you."

He lifted her from the chair, then sat down and cradled her protectively against his chest. Brushing his lips across her forehead, he whispered soothingly to her, patiently waiting for the storm to subside, trying not to fear the worst.

When she grew silent, he tipped her chin up to peer into her dark, haunted eyes. "Tell me what's wrong, sweetheart."

She inhaled a deep, shuddering breath and blurted hoarsely, "My father came to see me."

Quentin went rigid with shock. "*What!* When?"

And out came the harrowing story of the night she'd nearly died.

Quentin listened with a combination of shock, horror, sympathy and outrage. By the time she'd finished the devastating account, he was so visibly shaken that she laid a gentle hand over his galloping heart, as if to absorb his raging emotions back into her own body. Quentin would never lay a hand on a woman, let alone someone's mother. But the savage fury he felt toward Carlene Austin made him glad that she was nowhere near him, lest he be tested. And as for that son of a bitch Ray Austin, all bets were off.

"I'm so sorry, Lex," Quentin uttered fiercely as he palmed her face, brushing his lips over her damp cheeks and eyelids, kissing away her tears. "I'm so damn sorry you had to go through that. *All* of it."

"Me too," she murmured. "But at least now I know why I'm so afraid of heights. Even though I was only two, I had repressed memories of the trauma."

"God." Quentin shuddered at the thought of existing in a world without her in it. Unthinkable.

They sat there for a long time, just holding each other and whispering tender reassurances.

But hard, cold reality eventually intruded when Lexi's cell phone rang. Giving Quentin an apologetic look, she dug it out of her pocket and answered. After a brief conversation, she ended the call and drew a deep breath, as if to marshal her courage.

"That was my Realtor. She wants to show the house in an hour."

Dread lodged in Quentin's gut. His arms instinctively tightened around her. "You don't have to leave—"

"Let me go, Quentin."

Their eyes met, and he knew she wasn't just asking to be released from his arms.

He shook his head slowly. "I can't do that. I can't let you go. I told you that before."

"And *I* told you that this was something I needed to do!" she burst out desperately.

"Lex—"

"This place has become my own toxic wasteland, and no matter how hard I try to outrun the memories, they keep catching up to me. They're *poisoning* me, Quentin. So I need to go away for a while, and you need to let me."

His chest squeezed painfully. "How long?"

Her expression grew veiled. "I don't know. However long it takes."

She couldn't have hurt him more if she'd driven a stake

through his heart. His arms fell away from her, and she quickly climbed off his lap.

Too agitated to remain seated, he lunged to his feet. Lexi backed away from him, twisting the knife even deeper into his heart.

"Where are you planning to go?" he demanded. "Are you joining your brother and sister in New York? I'd rather not do a long-distance relationship, but if that's what it takes—"

"I'm not going to New York," Lexi said quietly.

"Then where...?" As comprehension dawned, the blood drained from his head and he stared at her. "*France?* You're going all the way to *France?*"

She swallowed tightly, then nodded. "I've applied for a faculty position at Le Cordon Bleu school in Paris. Their chef instructors are predominantly French, but given my teaching credentials and the early success of my cookbook, my prospects look...promising."

"In other words," Quentin snarled, "it's pretty much a done deal."

She just looked at him, her eyes silently pleading with him to understand.

But he couldn't. Maybe it was selfish of him, but he just *couldn't* accept her decision to walk out of his life.

"You don't have to do this," he told her.

"Yes, I do."

"No, you don't!" he exploded, his voice hoarse with desperation. "Stay here with me, Lexi. Let me help you work through this. You don't have to have any contact with your screwed-up parents. If your father comes anywhere near you, I'll kill him. And if you don't want to deal with your mother, we'll take out a restraining order against her. Hell, I'll draft it myself!"

Her expression softened. "You can't fix this for me, Quentin. Not this time."

Raw emotion clawed at his throat. "What about us? Doesn't our relationship matter to you?"

"Of course it does!" Her voice dropped from a shout to a pleading whisper. "You *know* how much you mean to me, Quentin."

"Then don't leave me!" he half commanded, half begged.

Tears glazed her dark eyes. "I need to do this. I *have* to do this. If you really love me—"

"*If?*" he thundered incredulously. "*If?* I've spent the past month—hell, the past *twenty years*—proving to you just how much I love you! Don't you *ever* use the words *if* and *love* in the same breath when it comes to my feelings for you!"

She lifted a trembling hand to her mouth, rapidly blinking back tears.

As Quentin glared at her, he was struck by an unsettling new thought. "This isn't just about your parents, is it?"

Lexi averted her gaze, saying nothing. But her silence spoke volumes.

Quentin took a small step toward her. "Are you having second thoughts about us?"

"No! Of course not." But she wouldn't look at him.

His tension mounted. "What's going on, Lex? When I left town a week ago, everything was great between us. What's changed?"

"Nothing. I just…" She trailed off with a helpless shake of her head.

"You just what?" Quentin prodded.

She exhaled a deep, shaky breath that ruffled her long bangs. "I don't know if I'm…secure enough to be with someone like you."

"Someone like me," Quentin repeated with forced calm.

She nodded, chewing her lower lip. "A man who can have any woman he wants. A man who's *used* to having any woman he wants."

Quentin frowned. "Lex—"

"I don't want to get hurt again, Quentin," she whispered. "I don't think I could survive it."

His chest tightened. "I'm not going to hurt you, Lex," he said with quiet urgency. "I *love* you. What more can I say or do to convince you of that?"

"I don't know!" Her eyes were filled with anguished confusion. "And that's part of the problem. You shouldn't *have* to keep trying to convince me. I shouldn't be wrestling with all these doubts about our relationship."

"But you are," Quentin stated flatly.

She swallowed hard, nostrils flaring as she fought back tears. "I just need time to get away and think…sort things out."

"What's there to sort out, Lex? Either you love me and want to be with me—or you don't."

She shot him a stricken look. "It's not that simple!"

"Bullshit! It *is* that simple when two people genuinely love each other!" He took another step toward her. "So tell me, Alexis. *Do* you really love me?"

"Of course I do!" she cried out. "How can you even question that?"

"The same way you can question my commitment to this relationship!" Quentin fired back. "After everything we've been through, after everything we've overcome this past month alone, I can't believe you still have doubts about whether I can be faithful to you!"

Guilt flared in her eyes before she glanced away, lips tightly compressed.

Quentin glowered at her, chest heaving up and down as he fought for composure. He was *so* damn tempted to haul her into his arms, kiss her senseless, bear her down to the floor and make love to her until she surrendered to his demands. But he didn't want to seduce her into staying with him. He wanted her to stay because she knew, beyond a shadow of a doubt, that she could trust him wholeheartedly. He wanted her to stay because she knew she couldn't live without him.

Just as he knew he couldn't live without her.

"You're running again," he said softly.

"I'm not running!" But her voice broke in contradiction.

The small velvet box in his pocket was burning a hole through his clothes. But he didn't pull it out. If she rejected his marriage proposal, it would kill him.

"Moment of truth," he murmured, something they used to tell each other to prompt the other into making a difficult decision.

Lexi swallowed visibly. "Quentin—"

"Moment of truth!"

They stared each other down, the space between them charged with so much tension it was suffocating.

Finally she whispered, "I'm leaving. I have to."

Quentin held her gaze a moment longer, then pivoted and strode from the living room.

She hurried after him. "Please understand, Quentin. *Please*—"

He paused at the front door, hand on the doorknob. "You know how you always used to tell me that one of these days I'd push you too far, and you wouldn't forgive me?" He turned and pointed a finger at her. "If you do this to us—*if you leave me*—I'll never forgive you."

And with those devastating words vibrating in the air between them, he slammed out of the house, knowing he'd seen it—and possibly her—for the last time.

Chapter 20

Paris. The city for lovers.

Probably not the best place to take refuge if one was nursing a broken heart. But Lexi had always been a glutton for punishment. So over the next four months, she immersed herself in the hustle and bustle of Paris, hoping the City of Light would help chase away the darkness ravaging her soul.

As she'd hoped, she'd been offered a chef instructor position at the prestigious Le Cordon Bleu school. While she waited for her summer classes to begin, she worked on her next cookbook, inspired by her surroundings. She moved into a studio apartment in the trendy, historic district of Le Marais. Many nights she sat on her balcony with a glass of champagne and quietly toasted the stars. She went for long strolls, meandering down streets lined with outdoor markets, boutiques, cafés and elegant restaurants. She went to the theater and the opera, and spent entire afternoons wandering around museums and art galleries.

But nothing was the same without Quentin.

Every time she saw an elderly French couple companionably walking arm-in-arm, she wanted to weep. Although she was only three hours away, she never visited Burgundy. It was hard enough trying to keep the memories at bay without actually being there.

She missed Quentin so much she ached. She would have given *anything* to hear his husky laughter, or to hear the excitement and passion in his voice as he told her about a new case. She missed his lazy smile, missed the way his eyes glinted wickedly when he looked at her. Every night she lay awake in bed for hours, craving the heat and strength of his body wrapped around her, buried deep inside her. And she couldn't help wondering, over and over again, whether she'd made the biggest mistake of her life by leaving him.

When she first arrived in Paris she'd tried to contact him, sending text messages and emails, playing their favorite songs on his voice mail.

He never responded.

After a while she'd given up, dismally realizing that she'd not only lost the perfect lover and companion. She'd lost her best friend.

One day she ventured to Asha's upscale boutique on the Champs-Elysees. Since becoming a grandmother, Asha had created a line of maternity and infant wear that had become very popular with many celebrity moms. Lexi wanted to buy some outfits for her goddaughter. Every time Reese emailed new photos of Savannah, Lexi was shocked to see how fast she was growing. And she felt guilty for missing out on so much.

She was standing in the boutique, fighting back tears as she gazed upon a beautiful maternity blouse, when an amused voice drawled, "Don't get tears on my merchandise, *chère,* or I'll have to charge you for it."

Startled, Lexi glanced around and was surprised to discover Asha standing there.

"Asha! I didn't know you were in Paris."

Asha chuckled. "Darling," she said, greeting Lexi with a double-cheek kiss, "when am I *not* in Paris?"

"Right. Of course." Asha's international haute couture house was headquartered there. She somehow managed to divide her time between Atlanta, New York and Paris—and still keep Sterling happy.

She arched a fine brow at the blouse Lexi was holding. "Is there a reason you're browsing through the maternity racks?"

Lexi blushed deeply. "I—I was just, um, looking around," she stammered, clumsily hanging up the blouse. "Everything you design is absolutely gorgeous."

Asha gave her a knowing smile, then took her hand and led her through the busy boutique to a private, luxurious reception area in the back. With barely a snap of her fingers, an assistant materialized out of thin air bearing two glasses of champagne on a silver tray.

"So, Alexis, are you enjoying your stay in Paris?" Asha asked, gesturing her to join her on an elegant silk sofa.

"Very much." Lexi smiled as she sat down. "It *is* Paris."

"Mmm. The last time you were here, you were moping over Quentin because he'd called to say he couldn't make it for New Year's." Asha smiled faintly. "And here you are again, *chère*, moping over Quentin."

Lexi flushed, averting her gaze to take a gulp of wine.

"He's not faring much better," Asha told her. "Michael says Quentin has become such a workaholic that even Marcus is worried. He says Quentin is often the first one at the office, and sometimes he's still there the next morning when Marcus returns." She heaved a dramatic sigh. "Looks like the hard-partying, skirt-chasing scoundrel we once knew and loved is no more."

Lexi said nothing.

After another moment, Asha said gently, "You don't belong in Paris, Alexis. You belong in Atlanta with Quentin. Or have you already forgotten my New Year's toast?"

That startled a laugh out of Lexi. "I haven't forgotten it," she said dryly. "I doubt that any of your guests have."

"Well, darling, I hope *they're* doing a better job of fulfilling it than you are."

Lexi's smile faded, and she let out a shaky breath. "It's complicated."

"Love always is." Asha took a languid sip of wine. "How's your mother doing?"

Lexi swallowed. "I don't know. I haven't spoken to her in months." She'd ignored all her mother's attempts to reach her, even when Carlene had left tearful, rambling messages begging Lexi to return home. She wasn't ready to let her mother back into her life. She didn't know if she ever would be.

Watching the play of emotions across her face, Asha murmured, "Your mother is a bitter, ignorant woman—"

Lexi bristled defensively. "Now hold on—"

"—who happens to love you very much," Asha finished quietly.

Surprised, Lexi stared at her.

Asha smiled ruefully. "We're not so very different, your mother and I. We both made the mistake of trusting the wrong men, and we allowed our mistakes to define the type of mothers we would become." She paused. "Someday you should ask Samara about the history of our relationship.

Ask her how she found it in her heart to forgive me for abandoning her."

Lexi regarded Asha for a long moment, then nodded slowly. "I will."

"Good." Asha touched her cheek. "Have you been back to Burgundy?"

Lexi shook her head. "I can't," she whispered.

Asha gave her a gentle, intuitive smile. "That's the thing about memories, *chère*. They follow you wherever you go. But not just the bad ones. The good ones, too."

Chapter 21

His was the first face she searched for when she arrived at the party.

When she found him, her heart skidded to a complete stop.

He was playing with Savannah, gently hefting her into the air and making goofy faces at her. The baby's delighted gurgles and squeals blended with his deep, rumbling laughter, a sound that was pure music to Lexi's starved ears.

Drawing a deep breath to shore up her courage, she started across the crowded room, which was filled with friends and family members who had gathered to celebrate Sterling's sixty-seventh birthday. Even as Lexi exchanged smiles and greetings, she kept her gaze trained on Quentin.

As she neared him, he turned and gently handed the baby to his mother, who'd been standing beside him awaiting her turn to hold Savannah.

From across the room, someone called out a boisterous greeting to Lexi. Quentin glanced up sharply, his gaze sweeping over the crowd. When he saw Lexi, those hazel eyes widened in surprise.

They stared at each other for the space of three breathless heartbeats before his expression grew shuttered and he glanced away.

As Lexi approached on rubbery legs, Georgina Reddick beamed a smile at her. "Alexis! Welcome home!"

Lexi smiled warmly. "Hello, Mrs. Reddick. It's good to see you." She hugged her, then kissed the top of Savannah's curly head before meeting Quentin's remote gaze.

"Hey," she said softly.

"Alexis," he murmured.

No smile, no hug for her. She might as well have been a stranger.

Seeking to cover the awkward moment, Georgina grinned at Lexi. "I know this is your goddaughter, but I've been patiently waiting to get my turn to hold her, so you can't have her yet."

Lexi laughed. "That's okay," she said, affectionately kissing the baby's chubby fist. "I spent the day with Reese and Michael yesterday, so Savvy and I already had our bonding time."

A flicker of surprise crossed Quentin's face.

Lexi had asked their friends not to tell him that she was back in town, because she was afraid that he'd skip the party just to avoid seeing her.

"How was Paris?" Georgina asked her.

"Good. But I—"

"Excuse me." Quentin abruptly departed.

Lexi watched him go, her heart constricting painfully. Her gaze returned to Georgina, who was regarding her with gentle maternal compassion. "I'm glad you're back, Alexis," she said quietly.

"Me too," Lexi whispered.

Georgina searched her face. "Are you staying?"

Lexi nodded. "Yes."

"Good." Georgina smiled down at the adorable, gurgling baby perched on her hip. "I'm ready to be a grandmother. Catch my drift?"

Lexi swallowed. "Yes, ma'am."

And with that, she went in search of Quentin, hoping and praying that he hadn't given up on her.

She found him outside in the gazebo that overlooked the huge, beautifully landscaped backyard. He stood at the balustrade staring out at the light drizzle that had kept the party indoors. He looked incredible, Lexi thought with an ache of deep longing. Breathtakingly virile in a black T-shirt and dark jeans that rode low on his hips, he was definitely a sight for sore eyes.

Pausing in the entrance to the gazebo, Lexi shoved her moist palms into the back pockets of her jeans. "Mind if I come in?"

"Free country," he murmured without turning his head.

She stepped forward, shaking with nerves. She could feel the tension radiating from his body, warning her to keep her distance. Leaning against one of the support columns, she gazed at him.

"I missed you," she said, husky with emotion.

He didn't respond.

"Not a day went by that I didn't think about you, wondering what you were doing, wondering what kind of cases you were working on, wondering what you ate for dinner. I missed cooking for you, I missed talking and laughing with you. I *missed* you."

He remained silent and impenetrable.

She forged ahead. "I had to leave, Quentin. I know it was hard for you—"

His head whipped around. *"Hard?"* he growled, his voice vibrating with suppressed fury. "You ripped my heart out of my damn chest and dangled it in front of my face. *Hard,"* he said mockingly, all but spitting the word at her feet before he turned away again.

She trembled at his harsh outburst, but she didn't back down. Too much was at stake. "Do you remember when I went to New York to attend culinary school? I was so excited because you'd been accepted into Columbia's law school, so that meant we'd still be together. But then you decided to go to Emory instead so you could keep an eye on your mother. I was so disappointed, but I understood and supported your decision."

A muscle clenched in his jaw. "It's not the same thing, and you know it."

"That's not the point I was trying to make." She took a tentative step toward him. "When I left for Paris, I told myself that we could make it work. I kept reminding myself that our friendship hadn't suffered while I was in New York and you were here. We were apart for a whole year, but we spoke on the phone every day. Whenever you'd gripe about some class that was kicking your butt, I'd make you laugh with a story about an embarrassing blunder I'd made at cooking school. And whenever I had doubts about whether I had the chops to become a chef, you'd encourage me and remind me what a great cook I was." She smiled poignantly. "We were always there for each other, so I knew we'd be okay."

Quentin fell silent again.

"That's what I counted on when I made the heart-wrenching decision to leave you and go to Paris. And make no mistake about it, Quentin. It was the hardest decision I've *ever* made in my life. If you don't believe that, then maybe you don't know me as well as I thought you did."

He shot her a dark glance that warned her not to pursue that line of thinking.

Her heart thumped into her throat. She swallowed tightly before continuing, "While I was in Paris, I did a lot of praying and soul searching. And one day I realized something. All these years, I'd always believed that my mother was the reason I came back to Atlanta after graduating from culinary school. I always thought I'd returned home out of a sense of obligation to her, and that same obligation was keeping me here." She shook her head slowly. "But I was wrong. It was you, Quentin. *You're* the reason I rushed back home all those years ago. And *you're* the reason I've stayed."

She watched, breathless, as he bowed his head and gripped the balustrade with trembling hands.

"I looked in the mirror," she continued softly, tears misting her eyes, "and I asked myself what I was doing in Paris when my heart was here with you. I *love* you. And it scares me to realize that maybe, just maybe, some of Adam's fears were founded. I'm not excusing his deplorable behavior, but the truth is that I've *always* loved you, Quentin. I don't know if I've been in denial all these years, or genuinely clueless. But my eyes are open now, sweetheart. And the greatest gift you could have ever given me was that kiss on the bal—"

He whirled suddenly, reaching her in two powerful strides and hauling her roughly into his arms. Her heart soared to the sky and she clung to him, wrapping her arms around his neck as tears of joy and relief streamed down her face.

"I love you, *love* you," Quentin whispered hoarsely. "Don't ever leave me again!"

"I won't!" she promised.

He hugged her tightly, then cradled her tear-streaked face between his hands and gazed fervently into her eyes. "I've always loved you, Lex. I wish to *God* I'd figured it out before you married another man. That was one of the worst days of my life!"

Her heart swelled with raw emotion. "I should have known that day how I truly felt about you," she confessed. "The moment I stepped through the church doors and started searching for you, I should have *known*."

Quentin groaned, his mouth covering hers with fierce, tender urgency. They kissed as though their very lives depended on it, pouring years of secret longing and passion into the kiss.

Drawing back slightly, Quentin rested his forehead against hers and stared into her eyes, into her soul. "Help me make this right, sweetness," he said in an achingly husky voice. "Say you'll marry me."

Smiling through her tears, Lexi reached up and cupped his warm cheek in her palm. "I thought you'd never ask."

Whooping with triumphant elation, Quentin lifted her into his arms and spun her around before capturing her lips in another deep, searing kiss that was eventually interrupted by the sound of applause.

Mouths parting reluctantly, they glanced toward the house. A crowd of their friends, Georgina Reddick and several other guests had gathered on the veranda, their faces wreathed in wide, delighted grins as they watched the emotional reunion.

"I *told* you Q would be next," Michael crowed to an incredulous Percy Sheldon. "Now pay up."

Laughter swept over the veranda.

"So are we having another garden wedding," Asha called out merrily, "or do you lovebirds have somewhere else in mind?"

Lexi and Quentin looked at each other and smiled. "Burgundy."

Epilogue

Three months later

Everything was perfect.

The weather was glorious. The hills surrounding the château were covered with fields of lavender that perfumed the air, mingled with the scent of ripe grapes wafting from the lush vineyards. Flowers bloomed in the beautifully manicured garden, where three hundred guests were gathered.

The flower girls sprinkled a trail of roses and anemones in honor of the bride's favorite print, a gift from the groom. Ring bearers Matthew and Malcolm Wolf drew adoring sighs and chuckles from the crowd as they strutted down the aisle. The gorgeous dresses worn by the bridesmaids— Reese, Samara, Raina, and Summer Austin—elicited hearty murmurs of approval.

An awed hush swept over the garden when the bride

made her entrance, radiant in a strapless princess gown fashioned out of white appliquéd silk. Handkerchiefs were fumbled out of purses and dabbed at watery eyes.

Everything was perfect.

But as Lexi started down the aisle on Sterling's arm, she only had eyes for Quentin. Not only was he devastatingly handsome in a custom-made Armani tuxedo, but the worshipful look in his eyes took her breath away. Over the years they had laughed and cried together, and fought like there was no tomorrow. But in Quentin's eyes she saw a *lifetime* of tomorrows, glorious days filled with joy and fiery passion. She saw the promise of the children they would bring into the world together. And most of all, she saw *love*. A deep, unshakable love that would sustain them through whatever trials life brought their way.

As they exchanged their vows on that momentous day, their voices trembled with emotion. This time when Lexi spoke the words "I do," she knew down to her soul that this was forever. When Quentin lifted her veil and gazed down at her glowing face, tears were swimming in both their eyes. As their lips joined in a passionate kiss, their guests showered them with cheers and applause.

As Quentin swept Lexi into his arms and carried her back down the aisle, she was surprised—and touched—to see her mother weeping with gratitude.

Carlene was undergoing counseling to deal with her emotional scars. After having a long heart-to-heart talk, she and Lexi had agreed to work on mending their relationship. They were taking things one day at a time, and Lexi believed that someday they would be all right.

But even if the painful memories from the past haunted them for years to come, Lexi knew that with Quentin by her side, she'd never have to run again.

* * *

Later, after sneaking out early from the reception festivities, the newlyweds lay blissfully sated in each other's arms after an explosive round of lovemaking that had left them shuddering and gasping for breath.

They were spending their first night as husband and wife in a cozy cottage located on the grounds of the estate. They would relocate to the château tomorrow, after their friends and family members had departed for home. When some of the other couples—namely Michael and Reese, Marcus and Samara, and Warrick and Raina—joked about sticking around longer to enjoy the scenic French countryside, Quentin wasted no time reminding them that they'd each had their romantic honeymoons, so now it was his and Lexi's turn.

At that moment, Lexi sighed contentedly and snuggled against him. "That had to be the most *beautiful* wedding in the history of weddings. And I'm not just saying that because it was ours."

Quentin smiled into her eyes. "And you had to be the most beautiful bride in the history of brides. And I'm not just saying that because you're mine."

"Oh, Quentin." Even as she smiled with pleasure, he could feel her blushing against his chest.

He'd meant every word. For as long as he lived, he would *never* forget the vision of Lexi wafting toward him in a hypnotic swirl of ivory silk. His heart had gotten so full it damn near burst out of his chest. He'd wanted to charge down the aisle and whisk her away before the ceremony even began. It must have showed on his face because Michael, standing beside him as best man, had murmured in a low, amused voice, "Easy, boy. Be patient."

Lexi was stroking Quentin's chest, a slow, gentle caress

that sent heat curling to his groin. He'd never get enough of making love to her. *Ever.*

"Asha designed all of our gowns," Lexi murmured. "I told her I wanted to look like a princess this time, because I was marrying my Prince Charming."

Quentin smiled softly. "Careful, sweetness," he warned. "You're gonna make me fall even harder for you."

"Good. I'm greedy."

He kissed her, a deep, possessive kiss that reminded her just how greedy *he* could be, too. As he drew back, she let out a soft, shaky breath and grinned.

"I'm not getting any sleep tonight, am I?"

He gave her a wolfish grin. "Or for many nights to come."

She pretended to consider this, then shrugged. "I can live with that."

They both laughed.

Cuddling her closer, Quentin laced his fingers through hers, and for a minute they just gazed at their joined hands with the matching gold wedding bands.

"Can you believe we did it?" Lexi marveled, sounding as awed as he felt.

"It's pretty incredible."

Lexi. His best friend.

His heart and soul.

His wife.

Would he ever get used to the knowledge that she was finally his? His to cherish. His to protect. His to love.

His for eternity.

It was enough to make a man shout to the heavens.

Lexi released another one of those soft, dreamy sighs. "I wish we could stay here forever, Quentin. Not even three weeks seem long enough."

"We'll come back," Quentin assured her.

"You promise?"

"Absolutely. After all—"

"—this is our spot," she finished tenderly.

They smiled at each other, then gazed out the open bedroom window just as fireworks erupted into the night sky, cascading over the château and illuminating the ballroom balcony where their journey had begun with a stolen kiss at the stroke of midnight.

* * * * *

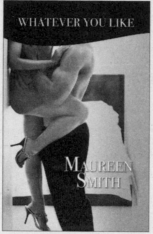

REQUEST YOUR FREE BOOKS!

2 FREE NOVELS
PLUS 2 **FREE GIFTS!**

KIMANI™
ROMANCE

Love's ultimate destination!

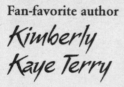